CORRESPONDENCE
An Adventure in Letters

Correspondence
An Adventure in Letters

a novel by

N. John Hall

David R. Godine
Publisher · Boston

First published in 2011 by
DAVID R. GODINE · *Publisher*
Post Office Box 450
Jaffrey, New Hampshire 03452
www.godine.com

LIBRARY OF CONGRESS CATALOGING-IN-PUBLICATION DATA

Hall, N. John.
Correspondence : an adventure in letters, a novel / by N. John Hall.
p.   cm.
ISBN 978-1-56792-412-1 (hardcover)
1. Retirees—New Jersey—Fiction. 2. Novelists, English—19th century—
Manuscripts—Fiction. 3. Novelists, English—19th century—
Correspondence—Fiction. 4. Auctioneers—England—London—Fiction.
5. Manuscripts—Expertising—Fiction. I. Title.
PS3608.A54745C67 2011
813'.6—dc22
2010014809

FIRST EDITION
Printed in the United States of America

FOR BOB CALL

Chapter One

Christie's
Books and Manuscripts
8 King Street, St. James's
London SW1Y 6QT

Mr Larry Dickerson
27 East 13th Street 2-B
New York, NY 10003
USA

12 October 2006

Dear Mr Dickerson,

Your letter to the president of Christie's London has been passed on to this department.

If the manuscript letters you are offering us are genuine, they are indeed worth a good deal of money. Could you send me more particulars?

Yours sincerely,
Stephen Nicholls
Books and Manuscripts

27 East 13th Street 2-B
New York, NY 10003

Mr. Stephen Nicholls
Books and Manuscripts
Christie's
8 King Street, St. James's
London SW1Y 6QT
U.K.

Oct. 19, 2006

Dear Mr. Nicholls,

   Of course the letters are genuine. Why else would I be trying to sell them? They're old and hard to read – though I am working on it.

                              Yours truly
                              Larry Dickerson

PS   Are you sure Christies is the right place for me to be selling these letters? Who is better at this kind of thing, you or the other place? Sotheby?

Christie's
Books and Manuscripts
8 King Street, St. James's
London SW1Y 6QT

Mr Larry Dickerson
27 East 13th Street 2-B
New York, NY 10003
USA

27 October 2006

Dear Mr Dickerson,

Please do not take umbrage, but authenticity is the first thing we must
verify beyond reasonable doubt before putting any autograph letters up
for auction. Can you send me a list of your maternal great-grandfather's
correspondents? Names and dates? Or, better yet, send photocopies of
the originals? We have to know what's in the letters, their content,
before coming to a decision about how to market them.

Yours sincerely,
Stephen Nicholls
Books and Manuscripts

PS It's Sotheby's – with an inverted comma and an s̲ at the end, just as
in Christie's. But we at Christie's can take care of your letters just fine.

27 East 13th Street 2-B
New York, NY 10003

Nov. 7, 2006

Dear Mr. Nicholls,

I can't say I blame you for being careful. Since writing to you a friend of mine at the bank has told me that many of the things you people deal with turn out to be questionable – forgeries in fact. People who work in banks know about forgeries. At least they are supposed to. These letters are the real deal. And there's quite a stack of them.

I'm making a complete list, but I can tell you right off the bat that I have letters from Charles Dickens, W. M. Thackeray, Charlotte Bronte, Anthony Trollope, George Elliot, Wilkie Collins, Thomas Hardy, and Samuel Butler. How's that for a line up? I myself don't claim to know anything about these people except that they are famous writers – although I never really even heard of Collins or Butler, but I gather that they are pretty famous, too.

Though I am about as American as you can get, my great-grandfather on my mother's side was an English bookseller. His name wasn't Dickerson of course, since he was on the female side. His name was Jeremy MacDowell. For my part, I think his letters are pretty important, too. And of course there is at least one letter from him for each letter from the writers he was so interested in. I hope his are also worth something. Another friend of mine says all the letters should be kept together and not "broken up." Is that right?

And why do you use the word "autograph"? <u>Of course</u> the letters are signed.

Yours truly
Larry Dickerson

PS Thanks on Sotheby's. We call them apostrophes over here, not "inverted commas" – kind of a funny way of naming them. After all, they are not commas – upside down or not.

Christie's
Books and Manuscripts
8 King Street, St. James's
London SW1Y 6QT

22 November 2006

Dear Mr Dickerson,

What you say about not breaking the set is spot on. Nonetheless, I must
tell you that if we were to sell each letter individually, the aggregate
would, in all likelihood, come to more money in the end. But the
process would take much longer. Moreover, serious collectors (which
include major libraries), the academic community, and Christie's itself
would much prefer that all the letters, both sides of the
correspondence, be kept together, and I applaud your implied decision
to do so. That said, I don't at all recommend selling everything in one
large batch, but rather in eight batches, or "lots" as we call them. That is
to say, we would keep all the Dickens letters (to him and from him)
together in one lot; all the Thackeray letters in another lot, etc. This will
make for eight lots rather than one huge lot, although the eight lots
would be sold consecutively as part of the same auction event. These
eight lots could be presented as your great-grandfather's papers, so to
say. If everything were combined into one lot, the price would prove
prohibitive for most buyers. But eight lots would mean that Dickens
collectors, for example, who are looking for Dickens material only,
would be able to bid on their man, and against each other, which
effectively drives up the price. Does this make sense?

Your great-grandfather's letters, sad to say, are basically worthless,
except as providing context and provenance for the other letters.
"Provenance" in the trade means where something comes from by way
of proving its authenticity.

> 5 <

In this business we use "autograph" to mean written in the hand of the person involved. Technically, each of the letters in your possession is an "ALS" for "autograph letter signed."

I look forward to hearing from you and receiving the list and, in due course, the photocopies.

Do you use email? It's much faster (and easier) than traditional letters. I am:

S.Nicholls@christies.co.uk

Yours sincerely,
Stephen Nicholls

PS   Perhaps "inverted commas" is somewhat misleading. But while they do not serve any comma-like syntactical function, from a printer's standpoint, they are in shape exactly that, inverted commas.

27 East 13th Street 2-B
New York, NY 10003

Dec. 2, 2006

Dear Mr. Nicholls,

I had email but it went on the blink. But my son is coming over from Jersey and he is a whiz at computers and will have me "up and running" by next week.

Yeah, we'll keep the letters in eight batches or "lots" as you call them. Makes sense, and I take your analysis all around. I won't make the bad pun and say I hope it also makes dollars and cents.

And I can tell you right now that what you fellows call the "provenance" is in this case right "spot on," as you also call it. The letters were tied by ribbons in little bundles – one bundle for Dickens, one for Hardy, etc. These bundles were kept in a wooden box and have descended to me, the sole surviving male heir in the direct line. Do you need more information on my great-grandfather? Suppose I adopt a shorthand here, calling him my ggf? Jeremy MacDowell sold books in London. I mean he had a book shop, he didn't sell them in the street. He had a son, and the boy grew up, got married, and had three kids. When their father died the oldest kid inherited the box and a lot of old books. Now this MacDowell had only one child, a girl. And this girl, named Pamela – that's my mother – met my father Harold Dickerson when he was in the U.S. Army in England during the War. They got married and came, naturally, to the States, and they brought with them her most valued possessions, namely the box and other papers and a lot of old books. I think the box came close to being thrown out somewhere along the line. At least that's the story I heard as a kid. But it didn't get thrown out and I have it. How's that for provenance? I am starting to feel that it's nice to have something that old, and that personal, as they say.

What's this about my great-grandfather's letters not being worth anything? I don't see that.

Thanks for the dope on "autograph." We're dealing with ALSs alright, about 200 plus of them. Half from my ggf.

By the time you get this I'll be
                    L.Dickerson@verizon.net

                              Yours truly
                              Larry Dickerson

From: S.Nicholls@christies.co.uk
To: L.Dickerson@verizon.net
8 December 2006

Dear Mr Dickerson,

I didn't intend to slight your great-grandfather. But it is the case that letters from the famous people who have written to him – Dickens, Thackeray, George Eliot (only one "l"), Trollope, et al are valuable precisely because they are from Dickens, Thackeray, and so on. These are eminent, famous writers. Frankly, I doubt anyone even knows your great-grandfather's name. That's no fault of his, of course. Most people aren't famous, even if they corresponded with famous people.

From what you tell me, Jeremy MacDowell was your great-great-grandfather.

Please send the list and the photocopies.

Yours sincerely,
Stephen Nicholls

PS MacDowell sounds like a Scottish name.

⟨⟩

From: L.Dickerson@verizon.net
To: S.Nicholls@christies.co.uk
Dec. 10, 2006

Dear Mr. Nicholls,

My God you're right. Great-great-grandfather. And I'm supposed to know how to count, having worked in a bank.

But look – I know those writers are famous. I'm not stupid. Let's not talk about how many people know who my gggf was or is. His letters are, for one thing, just as old as the others, and I'd think that goes for something. And he was the one who always started the exchange of letters. My great-great-grandfather, Jeremy MacDowell, is the one responsible. Dickens would not for the fun of it have just started writing to Jeremy MacDowell, Bookseller, Paternoster Row, London EC, would he? No, Dickens wouldn't have done that. My gggf started the whole business. We wouldn't be having our exchange of letters if it wasn't for him.

What's this about MacDowell sounding like a Scottish name? I'm in the dark about Scottish versus English. Like most people over here I don't know anything about Scottish people except that they are supposed to be cheap and eat a lot of oatmeal. Jeremy MacDowell worked in London is all I know. And when he got old and left the business, he lived by the shore in a place called Whitstable, which is in Kent, and which I found out is in <u>England</u>. That doesn't sound like a Scotsman to me. But it was all long ago.

Can you give me some idea of what I might gross from the sale if everything goes smoothly?

Yours truly
Larry Dickerson

PS   One "l" in Eliot. Got it.
"Et al"? Is that English for "etc"?   Let me know by email that this email got to you. I'm too old to entirely trust email.

From: S.Nicholls@christies.co.uk
To: L.Dickerson@verizon.net
11 December 2006

Dear Mr Dickerson,

Your email arrived in good order.

Yes, it was all long ago, and do forget my careless word about the name being Scottish, but you should know that sundry famous "Brits" whom many people and most Americans think of as "English" are in fact of Scottish descent; among Victorian writers the philosopher John Stuart Mill ("the Saint of Rationalism") and the renowned Victorian "Prophet" Thomas Carlyle come to mind. And a surprisingly large number of London publishers and booksellers were of Scottish descent in the Victorian era. At one time, a bit earlier, Edinburgh, Scotland, was known as "the Athens of the North."

And yes, Jeremy MacDowell is important for setting off the exchanges, as you put it. In fact, it would be helpful if you gave us his birth and death dates, if you have them, along with any other details you may know of him.

But the money is in the Dickens, Thackeray, and other famous writers. A letter could be worth £50 or £2000 (or more), depending on content. A simple acceptance from Dickens of an invitation to dinner, for example, is worth nowhere near the value of a letter from Dickens which has him, say, reflecting on one of his novels, or on his habits of writing, or revealing something highly personal or even sensational. So I fear we can give you no idea of what the letters might bring until I have names, numbers, and actual content. You will see the justice of this.

And, now that I think of it, something important and elementary strikes me. You do not have the originals of your great-great-grandfather's letters. (I can't bring myself to call him your "gggf.") His letters were sent in the post to the writers who responded. But recipients didn't return letters. (Nor do we today.) What you have are not originals but copies that the sender, your great-great-grandfather, made of his own letters before posting them, a not uncommon practice in those days, especially among people in trade. That these letters are copies can't help but lessen their value, somewhat.

And of course he wasn't your great-great-grandfather back then.

Yours sincerely,
Stephen Nicholls

PS To be exact, "et cetera" means "and the other things," while "et alii" means "and the other persons." I don't mean to sound like a pedant in answering your questions.

⌒⟶

From: L.Dickerson@verizon.net
To: S.Nicholls@christies.co.uk
Dec. 12, 2006

Dear Mr. Nicholls,

   Well, that is a shocker, about my gggf's letters being his own <u>copies</u>. But I take your word for it. And it makes sense. Unless my gggf specifically asked that his letters be returned to him, which seems a clumsy thing to ask and a kind of odd arrangement, to say the least. Okay, so my gggf's letters are copies of his own originals. But how much less value are these copies?
   You're pretty sharp about him not being my great-great-grandfather <u>back</u> then. But I just can't help calling him that.
   I found out that he was born in 1829 and died on April 27, 1904. So he lived to a ripe old 75, or almost 75, because I don't have his exact birth date. The year is close enough. Do you keep good records in England? If you need the exact date of birth, you could look it up, as we say in baseball over here. He became an apprentice to his father, the first MacDowell bookseller, and took over the business as a young man, or so the family story says. I think he actually did some publishing – just pamphlets. And these pamphlets – all this is according to my niece Sally who is a history buff and interested in our family history – the pamphlets were supposed to have been "radical," which meant – she tells me – giving people the vote and being against the Church of England. But we don't have any of the pamphlets, so I say the hell with them. In any case, he wrote to all these novelists, Dickens, Thackeray, et al, as I'm learning to say. He may have written to other writers, but if he did, either they didn't answer, or he felt they were not worth bothering with, and he didn't keep their letters – or his copies.

Suit yourself of course on gggf as shorthand. Less letters to type is how I see it.

Good news! I missed two letters going through them quickly – it's a pretty messy stack of papers, different sizes and folded every which way. But two – two short ones – are from Charles Darwin. I don't know anything about evolution except that I believe in it. I was one of the few people I know who was brought up without any religion. Most of my friends had to grow up and get into their twenties, approximately, before giving up religion. Of course some other people stay religious all their life after their parents get them started. It's like they get a vaccination shot against doubting religion or against doubting God. My parents just never mentioned the subject. One time I asked my father – we were driving in the car somewhere in New Jersey where I grew up – and I asked my father if there was a God. He said no one's sure, that some people believe in God and others don't. I said I wanted to know what <u>he</u> thought, but he wouldn't say. Just said you make up your own mind when you are older. Another time I heard him talking to my mother in the kitchen, and he said to her something like, "If we're not careful, he'll pick up God in the streets – like bad words." They both laughed. When I was old enough to talk more about this, this time with my mother, she said her family in England were Unitarians who years ago back there in the old country were called "Nothingarians" because you didn't have to believe nothing much or even anything to be a Unitarian. But with her, even that little bit slipped away. My old man – my father that is – he had been brought up a kind of half-baked Catholic but he quit in his teens. So there you have my "provenance." But it helps to explain me getting such a kick out of having two letters from Charles Darwin himself. One is very short, but <u>they're from him</u>. These two letters have me as excited as the whole pile of others put together – except of course for the money.

Yours truly
Larry Dickerson

PS Isn't email great? It lets you kind of carry on without much effort, like I was just doing about me and religion. I can type faster than I can write so I sometimes sort of just let fly.

I gather "in the post" means "in the mail." No answer required.

Thanks on "et al." I will keep my etc and et al straight from now on. At least I am not like some people working at the bank who spelled "etc" as "ect," and even said "and et cetera." Made you ashamed of being a banker. Did I tell you I recently retired from being a "personal banker"? I started as a teller – after a lot of dead end jobs after I dropped out of college. First, you're a junior teller, then a senior teller. What a bore. Really tedious. Did you ever notice that there are no old bank tellers? Only the young can take it. Then I became a kind of half-baked accountant. I worked my way up till I got to be a "personal banker" with a small little office of my own. At first I was opening up checking accounts, savings accounts, and certificates of deposit. By the end I was doing mortgages, closing home equity loans, etc. As a personal banker in the old days you had to do a lot of math, and checking up on people's credit rating was slow. Then, later, with computers you could check in a minute and find out that someone's credit was lousy, so you'd tell them they'll get a letter in the mail. It was not as bad as being a teller, but still a real bore. I retired the minute I turned 65. I figure I can make it on my pension and savings and Social Security – do you have Social Security in England? It's a pain in the neck when they take the money out of your paycheck, but later on it's nice to have some cash coming in regularly into your checking account every month. But this way, I mean, now I'm retired, I can really make a project of working on these letters. I know you'll be happy to hear that.

And don't say you're being a pedant. (I had to check out the word.) I'm willing to learn – for the most part. Looking up words in the dictionary is not my idea of excitement, to tell the truth. And while telling the truth I should add that when I do take the trouble to look up words, I always seem to be looking up the <u>same</u> words. Can't tell you the number of times I looked up "egregious." An egregious number of times. And of course I use the dictionary for spelling. I like to get my spelling straight. Foreign words throw me, and I'll pass on to you any foreign quotes from the letters, and I'll be grateful for your help in that department. I am the first to admit I'm not anything at foreign languages. But I understand that pretty soon practically all Europeans will know English, anyway, so what's the point, really? I always think of

England as being sort of separate from Europe. I mean when you hear Europe you think of Frenchmen, Germans, Italians, Spaniards, even Scandinavians. Have I left any out? But I suppose technically England is part of Europe. Must be, right? After all, it's just next door, even if it is an island.

I take your word for it about Scotland being important. I have no idea who John Stuart Mill was. Should I? As for the one you call a prophet, I don't want to hear about him. Enough crackpot prophets over here today. Ranting and raving on television and radio. Jesus freaks and New Age nuts (whatever exactly "New Age" is) and other fakers talking about "spirituality." Give me a break.

If ever you feel impatient with me and my ignorance of things in this field, remember that my old man was one of the troops who knocked out Hitler for you.

⌣⟶

From: S.Nicholls@christies.co.uk
To: L.Dickerson@verizon.net
15 December 2006

Dear Mr Dickerson,

That is indeed good news about the Darwin letters. But, to keep things in proportion, for literary people (and they are the chief collectors of manuscript letters) a substantial letter from Dickens would be worth more than a substantial letter from Darwin. Unless the latter threw new light on Darwin's theory; that would make a big difference. History of science scholars of course devour Darwin. But Dickens is more "collected." However, as I've said previously, content is all-important, regardless of the writer.

You ask about how much less are copies of letters worth vis à vis the originals. A lot less. Copies are sometimes made hurriedly and inaccurately. They are, at bottom, not the "real thing," not actual "letters." Of course, since even the actual letters of Jeremy MacDowell are worth very little to begin with, this lessening in value doesn't add up to much. It's not quite like taking nothing from nothing, but fairly close. What MacDowell's letters do, of course, is supply <u>context</u>, and that is very important in these sets of exchanges. We – you – are fortunate indeed that Jeremy MacDowell made these copies. He must have been quite meticulous.

Any other surprises?

Yours sincerely,
Stephen Nicholls

Thanks on Hitler.

Your PSs are becoming as long as the bodies of your letters. Just an observation, not a complaint.

I do think we have arrived at the time when you must send us either photocopies or the originals for inspection.

From: L.Dickerson@verizon.net
To: S.Nicholls@christies.co.uk
Dec. 20, 2006

Dear Mr. Nicholls

    Honestly I still hesitate at this point to send you xeroxes – that's what we call photocopies over here. For one thing, another friend of mine – I have more than one or two of course – said that the bright electric light in the xerox machine might not be good for the old ink on the letters.
    No more surprises. I have been working on the project, starting with

lists and dates of letters to and from my ancestor. Some of the dates are tough to figure out.

Yours truly
Larry Dickerson

PS   You using the word "regardless" reminded me that when I was growing up in New Jersey, we were told to be careful not to say "irregardless," as if that one little slip could mark you off as a jerk. It was like people from Jersey City slipping up and saying "goil" for "girl." Or "terlet" for "toilet."

As for my long PSs, I guess I'm just a long PSer.

From: S.Nicholls@christies.co.uk
To: L.Dickerson@verizon.net
21 December 2006

Dear Mr Dickerson,

The light from the photocopier is not going to harm a letter from the mid-nineteenth century. We're not dealing with the Magna Carta here or even the Declaration of Independence. Letters from Dickens, Thackeray, George Eliot, et al are photocopied all the time.

I can see that you want the pleasure of being the first to see what's in these letters, and, frankly, I can't altogether blame you. They are yours. However, you should know that it's quite irregular for me to be discussing items I have not seen. So do what you feel you must and get the originals to me as soon as possible thereafter.

Yours sincerely,
Stephen Nicholls

From: L.Dickerson@verizon.net
To: S.Nicholls@christies.co.uk
Dec. 21, 2006

Dear Mr. Nicholls

You're probably totally right about the xeroxing, for all I know. I suppose I am really just trying that out as an excuse with you. The truth is I want to take on figuring out these letters on my own. Please try and understand that. Okay, so maybe my case is not the usual one — maybe it's a little "irregular." Maybe I'm peculiar, but that's how I feel about it.

Yours truly
Larry Dickerson

From: S.Nicholls@christies.co.uk
To: L.Dickerson@verizon.net
22 December 2006

Dear Mr Dickerson,

I shall for the immediate present rest contented with a carefully got-up list of the letters (with dates), and in due course summaries of the contents of the letters. I am coming to understand, or at least trying my best to understand, your wish to be the first in well over a century to read these manuscript letters. That is your choice, and I will respect your wishes. Still, bear in mind that the sooner you send the originals, the sooner you'll come into what I presume will be a tidy sum of money.

Yours sincerely,
Stephen Nicholls

From: L.Dickerson@verizon.net
To: S.Nicholls@christies.co.uk
Dec. 23, 2006

Dear Mr. Nicholls

Thanks for understanding me wanting to be the first to read these things. When I think that these letters have probably <u>never</u> been read since God knows when, I am hesitant to let them be seen, even by experts like yourself, at this point in time. Don't go thinking of me as a dog in a manger — I have learned that that is some kind of English expression for someone who feels he must have it all or no one will get any. Why it's a dog in a manger I don't get.

I sure hope it's a "tidy sum."

I'll try to get the list to you asap.

I'm going to try reading some of the books by my authors. When I was in high school we read The Tale of Two Cities and Silas Marner — Dickens and George Eliot (with one l) — and that was it for me as far as the writers on my great-great-grandfather's list goes. And frankly that was quite enough of that kind of heavy reading for me. In college — I was supposed to be an accounting major, but I only went one year — I didn't bother with anything in English except composition, and I was not too fond of that, either. I suppose you could say I'm one of those people who don't know anything about books but know what they like. I've been known to read a book or two now and then. But I am not so sure I'm really going to like reading much of these fellows. Some of them are actually girls. I mean women. I suppose that's neither here nor there. But I'm going to give them all a try.

Now that I mention it, the two women writers on my list used men's names. Charlotte Bronte used Currer Bell on her books, and George Eliot was really Marian Evans or Mrs. George Henry Lewes. You can see I've been reading up.

Actually, I realize I need to correct myself on something right away. I don't really have letters from Charlotte Bronte herself but letters to and from someone called Mrs. Gaskell, and they are letters about Charlotte Bronte. Charlotte Bronte was already dead when my gggf started writing these letters. That's a shame because Charlotte Bronte's Jane Eyre made her very famous, and everyone who watches TV or goes to the movies knows about Jane Eyre. I made the mistake of saying I had letters from Charlotte Bronte because at the top of these letters my gggf has written in pencil the name "Charlotte Bronte," and I hadn't gotten to look at the actual letters yet. But the letters are to and from this Mrs. Gaskell. I don't suppose those are worth much. I had to look her up in an old biographical dictionary which calls her an "authoress and the biographer of Charlotte Bronte." I'm a novice on all this stuff and I welcome all your suggestions.

Yours truly
Larry Dickerson

I realize this is Christmas holidays time, so take your time in answering.

From: S.Nicholls@christies.co.uk
To: L.Dickerson@verizon.net
2 January 2007

Dear Mr Dickerson,

I did know that Currer Bell and George Eliot were names used by women. Mrs. Gaskell's letters are far from worthless.

Another small point: we don't use "authoress" anymore. The word is considered demeaning or at least condescending to women. This is true in England and I'm sure (even more so) in the States. Similarly we try not to use the word "man" when we mean man or woman. "Person" is often a good substitute, as in "Chairperson." And we never use the word "poetess." It's a shame you don't have any poets. Tennyson and

Browning are the big nineteenth-century English names. Although, since your concern is largely in the eventual money these letters will bring you, I can tell you that novelists are decidedly "in" today as far as collectors go. Your great-great-grandfather was prescient in that regard.

Yours sincerely,
Stephen Nicholls

I believe the idea is that a dog in a feeding trough for cattle can't eat the hay himself, but he won't let the cattle in to eat it either. The expression wouldn't apply to you in any case because you are in fact eating the hay.

I don't get much time off for Christmas – the 25th, of course, and then Boxing Day.

From: L.Dickerson@verizon.net
To: S.Nicholls@christies.co.uk
Jan. 3, 2007

Dear Mr. Nicholls

"Prescient" is very good. For me, a dictionary word.

I'll take your word on authoress being non politically correct and won't use it anymore. Can I use waitress? Not that there are any waitresses in my letters here. But you say we're not supposed to use "man" words, only "person" words? Horsepersonship? Unsportspersonlike? Great.

And nope, no poets on my list. Besides, I don't care a rat's ass for poetry. Excuse the French.

Of course I'm counting on the money, but now that I'm involved, it isn't just the money, really.

The list. Did I tell you that all of my great-great-grandfather's letters – copies as you informed me – are dated, but not all the answers from the big guys are dated. You'd think if these famous people were going to take the trouble to write a letter in answer to my gggf that they would put the date on the damn thing, wouldn't you? But of course we can figure out an approximate date. After all, if someone — let's say Thomas Hardy — is answering a letter from my gggf (for which we have a date) we can tell that Hardy's letter wasn't written <u>before</u> that date, can't we? And probably pretty soon afterwards. If my gggf asks him a question and gets an undated answer, you wouldn't expect the answer to be written years later.

Just for an example, here's what we are dealing with. On June 28, 1861 my gggf writes to Dickens and tells him how pleased he was to meet him, even if only briefly, at what looks like the "Garrich Club" two nights ago. It seems my gggf was a guest there of a member, a fellow named Robert Bell. Then my gggf goes on to ask Dickens if he can ask a few questions about his novels. He says he would like to get Dickens's own position on a couple of things — I suppose we would say today that he wants it from the horse's mouth. My gggf wants to know whether he, Charles Dickens, thinks his later novels are really much "darker" than the early ones — like the critics are saying. And he wants to know if CD over the years has grown more pessimistic about human nature, etc. Is that etc okay? He asks about wasn't there more "comic" stuff in the early novels. Well, that is a pretty nervy thing to write, isn't it? I guess he figured the worst he could get was Dickens either saying he doesn't discuss such things, or, more worse, no answer at all. That's the kind of letters I am trying to "transcribe" and then to summarize as best I can for you. I know, Dickens's reply — that's what you really want to hear about. But remember it's only Dickens's <u>first</u> reply. He pretty much says yes, nice to have met you but that he seldom goes into such matters even with close friends. Not a very long letter, and not a very good start for my gggf trying to get writers to unbutton to him and trying to get the inside dope out of them. So, as I was saying, this first letter from Dickens wasn't a very good start. But then my gggf — as you will see — was not a man to get discouraged easily. He comes right back with a second letter — full of apologies for butting in, but asking practically the same questions all over again. And this time Dickens answers in a long letter that does go into the questions my gggf asked. But I am getting ahead of myself. Rest assured I am putting your list together. Names and dates – or as I say in some cases approximate dates – are all done, for the most part. But it's too early for me to summarize the contents. Contents requires a good deal of decoding the handwriting and references – what you call "context." Getting these straight will be a big project. I am plugging away. Will send the list by mail tomorrow.

Yours truly
Larry Dickerson

I'm glad I'm not a dog in a manger "in any case." That's a relief.

What in god's name is Boxing Day?

⌣⟶

From: L.Dickerson@verizon.net
To: S.Nicholls@christies.co.uk
Jan. 4, 2007

Dear Mr. Nicholls

The list is in the mail.

We got 18 from Dickens, 16 from Thackeray, 6 from that Mrs. Gaskell about Charlotte Bronte, 19 from George Eliot – well sort of from her – as you will see from the actual list most are from her "husband" George Lewes. Wilkie Collins, 9. From Trollope we have 13 and from Hardy a cool dozen (as we put it over here), and then 14 from Samuel Butler – I still don't know who that is. And the 2 from Darwin.

You add up all these numbers and you get 109 "famous" letters, and then you double that for the letters from my gggf, and it comes to 218, and then you add at least a dozen of my gggf's letters not answered – usually the last letter to the famous writer. Maybe the famous person got tired of answering questions or maybe he died. I am going to look up all the dates concerned. In fact I mean to check out just about everything I can about this business.

I figure roughly 230 letters in all.

My gggf's letters here may be only copies, as you say, but they still look like letters to me. Some of the letters <u>to</u> him are short. Others are quite long, or longish, as I understand you sometimes say over there in England.

Yours truly
Larry Dickerson

Chapter Two

INTEROFFICE MEMO

From   Stephen Nicholls   Books and Manuscripts
To   Robert Osborne   Office of the President
5 Jan 07

Bob,

I have been following up on the American, Larry Dickerson, whose
letter to you was passed on to me some time ago. He has what are by
his description letters from the some of the best-known Victorian
writers: Dickens, Thackeray, George Eliot, Mrs. Gaskell (on Charlotte
Brontë), Trollope, Collins, Hardy, Butler, and, a bit of an oddity in a list of
novelists, Darwin, roughly 110 letters. All the letters are to our American
friend's great-great-grandfather, a man named Jeremy MacDowell. And,
remarkably, all MacDowell's own letters to these worthies exist in copy.
I have had my assistant check on MacDowell, and there was indeed a
small bookseller of that name, operating out of Paternoster Row back
in the latter half of the nineteenth century. I haven't seen the originals
yet because Dickerson insists on making his own transcriptions first.
But from what he has told me so far, they do sound highly interesting –
and valuable. I trouble to tell you this only because I know the
Victorians used to be your specialty, or one of your specialties. I'll let
you know what we really have when I see the letters themselves. If all
goes well, we may have an interesting Victorian thing going on here in
manuscripts.

Stephen

_____

INTEROFFICE MEMO

From   Robert Osborne   Office of the President
To   Stephen Nicholls   Books and Manuscripts
5 Jan 07

Stephen,

Thanks. Always glad to hear of Dickens, Thackeray, etc. How come you
haven't seen the originals at least in photocopy? I don't like to interfere,
you know that. But I don't think you should be dealing with a client so
unforthcoming as this fellow — on company time.

Bob

_____

INTEROFFICE MEMO

From   Stephen Nicholls   Books and Manuscripts
To   Robert Osborne   Office of the President
6 Jan 07

Bob,

Some time ago I agreed that Dickerson would transcribe and
"annotate" everything first. The process, for me, has been like landing a
big fish, playing with him, giving him line, getting the net ready; this
rather than pulling him in immediately and risking breaking the line,
which in our case would be his taking his material across the street to
Sotheby's or privately to some millionaire.

In New York there is a Trollope collector, a retired Wall-Streeter, rich
as Croesus, of whom it is said that he is 1) a wonderful person, and

2) willing to spend on his man. I would think that in due course he will be bidding on Dickerson's Trollope letters. I can't imagine Dickerson ever heard of him. I believe we can trust Dickerson. And, truth to say, dealing with him has become enjoyable — it's dealing with someone completely new to the field who has an amateur's enthusiasm for the subject and who is making remarkably rapid progress.

Stephen

⌒

INTEROFFICE MEMO

From   Robert Osborne   Office of the President
To   Stephen Nicholls   Books and Manuscripts
6 Jan 07

Stephen,

Nice about the progress. But my thought is that you insist on seeing the originals or at least photocopies now. If that doesn't work — and let's not worry about Sotheby's or some millionaire — tell him that for the time being you can keep up only a strictly private email connection with him, i.e., off company time. I wouldn't suggest this if you did not say you enjoyed working with him. When he is ready to do actual business, you can welcome him (and his originals) back to Christie's.

Bob

⌒

INTEROFFICE MEMO

From   Stephen Nicholls   Books and Manuscripts
To   Robert Osborne   Office of the President
6 Jan 07

Bob,

Will do.

Stephen

Chapter Three

From: Nicholls@btinternet.com
To: L.Dickerson@verizon.net
6 January 2007

Dear Mr Dickerson,

Thanks for the list. It is very impressive. And what you tell me of the first exchange really whets my appetite to see the full-length originals.

I know we came to a kind of informal agreement that you would first work out the transcriptions; but if you change your mind and decide to let me have photocopies, we might work on them together. But in the meantime my boss decrees that I not continue our correspondence on company time until you send us originals. However, he thinks it fine that you and I stay in touch informally until such time as you have completed your transcribing and annotating, and return to Christie's with the originals. I personally think this should work well. For the time being, therefore, please address me at home:

Nicholls@btinternet.com

I have come to enjoy our email correspondence very much and look forward to its continuance – off company time.

Yours sincerely,
Stephen Nicholls

PS It's "Garrick Club," named after the actor David Garrick.

"Boxing Day" is December 26, on which day people give gifts to their help, postmen, servants (the few that have them), and so on.

⌣⌐

From: L.Dickerson@verizon.net
To: Nicholls@btinternet.com
Jan. 7, 2007

Dear Mr. Nicholls

Yeah, informal footing, that's fine. And I know what it's like when the boss puts his oar in. You'll be a private citizen till I am ready to deliver. We can be pen pals.

Thanks but no thanks on the help in transcribing. As I said earlier, I want to tackle this business on my own, first. It's a challenge. It's much more of a challenge than being a "personal banker," I can tell you. Here I am in my later years – just turned 65 some time ago as I may have told you when talking about Social Security – and I have a job before me that is challenging but also fun, and it may have a big pay off. Please try to understand.

Did I tell you that some of the Thackeray letters have drawings on them?

Yours truly
Larry Dickerson

Garrick Club. Got it. Thanks.

Boxing day. I must be the only American who knows what the hell that is.

⌣⌐

From: Nicholls@btinternet.com
To: L.Dickerson@verizon.net
8 January 2007

Dear Mr Dickerson,

That's very good news, about the drawings. One surprise after the other. Thackeray's sketches enhance the value of a letter greatly. He at one time wanted to be an artist, as you may know or are just coming to know. As a young man he hoped to illustrate Dickens's <u>Pickwick Papers</u> after the original illustrator went into his backyard and shot himself (immediately after Dickens found fault with his drawings). But Dickens chose another young artist, Hablôt Browne ("Phiz"). Ten years later Thackeray did do his own illustrations for <u>Vanity Fair</u>. I must say I'm eager to see your drawings.

Yours sincerely,
Stephen Nicholls

From: L.Dickerson@verizon.net
To: Nicholls@btinternet.com
Jan. 9, 2007

Dear Mr. Nicholls

   Glad you like it that the Thackeray letters have drawings. I'll send along a couple of my own tracings of the drawings by regular mail.

                                        Yours truly
                                        Larry Dickerson

   Why do you underline Vanity Fair and Pickwick Papers? I thought underlining was for emphasis. In college I sat next to a guy who underlined everything in the textbook – he used a yellow marker or pen of some sort. I used to tell him for God's sake what's the sense of underlining <u>everything</u>. But he kept doing it. Not that I got more than he did out of the class by not underlining anything. I told you college was not for me.

⟨—⟩

From: Nicholls@btinternet.com
To: L.Dickerson@verizon.net
9 January 2007

Dear Mr Dickerson,

Please don't trace Thackeray's sketches. It could damage them. Send photocopies.

Yours in haste,
Stephen Nicholls

By a long-standing convention, underlining (or italics) is used not only for emphasis but for the names of books and magazines. But you are quite correct in regard to excessive underlining for emphasis. It is much frowned upon by today's writers. Queen Victoria, who wrote thousands of letters, loved to underline for emphasis, so much so that after her death, when many of her letters were published, it became a kind of standing joke. I know her underlining firsthand, because we sometimes handle her letters.

⟨—⟩

From: L.Dickerson@verizon.net
To: Nicholls@btinternet.com
Jan. 11, 2007

Dear Mr. Nicholls

So okay, I won't trace the drawings. I was planning on being very careful, but as you seem to think it's dangerous I won't. I'll get them to you untraced somehow. I called my son, who is a hotshot with computers. He says he will be able to "scan" the drawings or photograph them and show me how to attach these to an email and send them over to you electronically. This may all take some time. But when you do get them, my advice is, Don't show them to anyone – except maybe another expert like yourself. I hope they will add to the excitement we hope to create when the whole business comes out. Most of the drawings are self portraits of "Your obedient servant," as Thackeray calls himself.

Your obedient servant
Larry Dickerson

I'll watch my underlining – names of books and magazines. Italics I don't bother with.

⌐‿⤳

From: Nicholls@btinternet.com
To: L.Dickerson@verizon.net
12 January 2007

Dear Mr Dickerson,

I look forward to seeing the Thackeray drawings in due course. You can be sure they will add cachet to his letters.

Stephen Nicholls

From: L.Dickerson@verizon.net
To: Nicholls@btinternet.com
Jan. 12, 2007

Dear Mr. Nicholls

Let's hope they add cash, too.

Something else dawns on me, namely that since we're moving along so nice, suppose we two people move to a more informal footing in our letters. In my gggf's time, if I had been writing to you for a time and got to know you, it would be "Dear Nicholls" or even "My dear Nicholls." No Mister, no first name. That much I have learned from the letters them-selves. Now we have never met, that's true. But we are writing so many letters back and forth that I think we should think about moving on to a first name basis in these letters – or, from the Victorian way of thinking, we are close enough for a last name only basis. What do you think?

Yours
Larry

From: Nicholls@btinternet.com
To: L.Dickerson@verizon.net
12 January 2007

Dear Larry

Yes, fine, and please call me Stephen. The last-name-only as a sign of intimacy went out years ago, or I'd gladly call you "My dear Dickerson."

All best
Stephen

From: L.Dickerson@verizon.net
To: Nicholls@btinternet.com
Jan. 13, 2007

Dear Stephen

Good.
Now along the lines of the cash, can you give me as we say in
baseball a ballpark figure? Can't you on the basis of the list give me
some vague idea how much the whole thing is worth? I won't hold you
to the figure. We've got about 110 autograph signed famous letters and
six Thackeray drawings and about 120 or so letters from my gggf (yes, I
know, copies).

                                                                Yours
                                                                Larry

From: Nicholls@btinternet.com
To: L.Dickerson@verizon.net
14 January 2007

Dear Larry

About the potential price, or what we call estimates, because, of
course, an auction house cannot guarantee a price: sometimes a single
really good Dickens letter will bring two thousand pounds, and of
course pounds are worth more than dollars, i.e., the exchange rate
currently favours the pound, which some believe will someday soon be
worth almost two dollars. The pound/dollar price fluctuates daily, as
you know. We could be talking anywhere from a barebones £10,000
(roughly $20,000) to – I can't say – ten or fifteen or twenty times that,

or even more. But until we know the contents by seeing photocopies, these are no more than guesses, educated guesses, I hope, but guesses nonetheless. Moreover, they are the very kind of thing my boss would not at all want me to be making without seeing the actual letters.

Auction houses like ours do set a cutoff point, called a "reserve," and if the bids don't go above that, the "lot," as we call it, doesn't sell.

Do you have insurance on the letters?

Best
Stephen

PS I know of course what a "ballpark" figure means, but baseball is utterly beyond me. I cannot understand baseball because in England we play cricket, and while some of the terms (innings, runs) are the same, they have different meanings in the two sports.

From: L.Dickerson@verizon.net
To: Nicholls@btinternet.com
Jan. 15, 2007

Dear Stephen

    About the "reserve" and all that, I suppose that is the way it works. You don't guarantee anything except that if the price that the bidders with their paddles come up with is less than the minimum "reserve," you call off the auction. I've got that straight, right? (And those mysterious telephone bidders — how do you know they're legit?) So if for one "clump" — the Dickens letters, for example — we set a minimum reserve of $100,000 — hoping to get twice that of course — and if the highest bid is only $50,000 it's no sale, and we are back to square one. Seems like a lot of trouble but I see your point. We don't want to be giving them away, do we? By the way, what is Christie's cut? I understand you are not selling them for me for nothing.

No, I never gave insurance any thought. A wealthy man I kind of met at the bank – a very nice guy – once said that he didn't "believe in" insurance except for liability for cars – which you have to have anyway – and maybe for your house. I live in a rented apartment. I figure insurance on most things is just money thrown away. I take my chances in that department.

Yours
Larry

PS I once saw some cricket played on Channel 13 and I couldn't make any sense of it, so I don't at all blame you the other way round. So on that score we're even. Baseball used to be our "national pastime," as they say, but now it's football. But old timers like myself love baseball. We grew up listening to it on the radio and on TV. But I'll try not to fall into baseball lingo.

From: Nicholls@btinternet.com
To: L.Dickerson@verizon.net
16 January 2007

Dear Larry

Christie's charges a seller's premium, or selling charge, on a sliding scale, with charges starting at 20% for lots up to £1000; the percentage moves downward as the price of a lot rises. However, this vendor's commission is often enough negotiable. It is much too early to be more specific at this stage. (There is also something called a buyer's premium starting at 25% up to a threshold of £25,000 and sliding down to 12% on lots over half a million pounds. But you need not at all concern yourself with buyer's premiums.)

We have not seen the actual letters yet, but your Dickens estimates are high. These are not Shakespeare letters. Still, you might think again about insuring your letters until you send them here.

Best
Stephen

Don't be shy of using baseball metaphors. I'm willing to learn.

⌣⌐

From: L.Dickerson@verizon.net
To: Nicholls@btinternet.com
Jan. 17, 2007

Dear Stephen

     You don't have to tell me Shakespeare is a hotter item than Dickens. Or Anthony Trollope. Such a name. I was just using these figures to have round numbers to work with.
     I guess I'm just a gambler, and so I'm not going to bother with insurance. The letters have lasted 150 years without insurance. What's another few months?
     That starting 20% sounds pretty high. But as we always say, you can't fight city hall. And you don't say how far it slides down. Let's hope we can do some tall "negotiating" when the time comes.

                                        Yours
                                        Larry

Chapter Four

From: L.Dickerson@verizon.net
To: Nicholls@btinternet.com
Feb. 24, 2007

Dear Stephen

You haven't heard from me in a few weeks but that doesn't mean I am not working. Full speed ahead. I'm transcribing, reading novels mentioned in my letters, looking up "context," and, big surprise, going to college.

Well, not really going to college – too late for that. But I'm taking a course at the New School – a funny name for a place that is really a college and has been around here nearly a century. But the New School is famous for its "Adult Education" or "Continuing Ed" courses in the evenings. The place is on West 12th Street, just around the corner practically from where I live. When I saw they were offering a course called "The Victorian Novel as Autobiography," I signed up, just in time for the first session.

I'm loving every minute of the course. It's terrific. I sort of went in thinking it would be a drag but something I should do to pick up some know-how on my writers. Well, the damndest thing, it's not a drag at all. Of course, this isn't a regular kind of college course, to say the least. No papers to write, no exams, no credits, no grades. And the people are coming to the course just because they like the Victorian novel. Most of them are already college graduates. We even have a lawyer – or two, I can't tell for sure. Truth is I can't wait for 6:30 on Tuesday nights to come around. The main point as I can see it so far is that almost all fiction has plenty of autobiography in it. (The other side of the coin is that all straight autobiographies are basically fiction – but we are sticking to novels.) So we are going to read these novels not only by themselves but in connection with the authors' lives.

My instructor – we don't usually call them "professors" at the New School – is a man named Irving Gross, and he really seems to know what he is talking about. And in addition to that, he is interesting <u>and</u> funny. The class is already crazy about him, and it's my guess that the women in the class (it's two thirds women) are all in love with him. I suspect he's quite the ladies man, as we say over here. But in any case this fellow seems to know his stuff.

More in my next letter.

Yours
Larry

A little more right here. This New School adventure of mine makes me think that maybe I should have tried harder and stayed in college and been an English major. But that's water over the dam, as they say. Speaking of English majors reminds me of Garrison Keillor – ever hear of him over there in the UK? He always makes jokes about "English majors." I think the idea is that English is a pretty useless degree unless you want to be an English teacher, and that's a thankless job to say the least. I remember back in the sixties when they were having all the protests and troubles and college students getting arrested and shot at, you'd notice in the news that the faculty member egging the students on was always from the English department. I was talking to one of my fellow "students" at the New School about this – we're too old to be students, really – and he said that maybe it was that English professors didn't have much of a subject and so they had time on their hands to lead the protests, etc. That kind of thinking is really unfair, because English professors do have a subject – books like <u>Great Expectations</u> and <u>Vanity Fair.</u> (I am watching my underlining.) Some people think that because they themselves can read <u>Great Expectations</u> they know pretty much as much about it as some professor does. Gross, in one of his asides (and he makes plenty of these) made a somewhat similar point about writing. He has this theory from a woman by the name of Shirley Hazzard (dangerous?). The idea is that everybody who is "reasonably literate" has a sneaking suspicion that they too could be a writer if they just put their mind to it. That, according to Gross, is as silly as a grown person who likes music suddenly deciding to become a concert violinist with the New York Philharmonic just because he can whistle a tune. People are smart enough to know that they couldn't just with a little effort become a concert violinist because they know they can't play the violin <u>at all</u>. But they can talk and write English, so they think that with a little concentration and enough free time, they could become writers. Fat chance, says Gross. He says that here in New York City if you look around at all the thousands of tall apartment buildings, it's a good bet that on every floor there is a wannabe writer with the unpublished manuscript of a novel or two in their desk drawer. And that's just where these things belong. We shouldn't call them novels, he says, till they get <u>published</u>, which'll be never. A good novelist is <u>far</u> rarer than a good concert violinist. And the would-be poets are even sillier. Sure, they can club together and "publish" their own stuff – Gross calls these writers "the mimeograph set" though nobody hardly knows what mimeographs are anymore, but you get the point. And now there is self publishing and all sorts of "computer generated" books – just another version, he says, of the oldfashioned "vanity press" – that being something I never heard of till now. Gross gives his view that in any language there can be no more than half a dozen or so really good poets <u>per century</u>. People think that writing poetry is easier than writing novels because poems are shorter, sometimes just, say, 14 lines or even less, and also because "the lines don't have to go to the edge of the paper." This last idea about poetry was not Gross's but some philosopher he quoted, whose name I forget. Doesn't matter.

Forgive me carrying on with these "lucubrations" – a word I picked up from Trollope. But as you can see, this New School course has me revved up.

From: Nicholls@btinternet.com
To: L.Dickerson@verizon.net
25 February 2007

Dear Larry

Nice to have your news filled with such enthusiasm for your course.
Excuse this lapidary reply — I'm frightfully rushed at the moment.

Best
Stephen

The philosopher's name was Jeremy Bentham.

From: L.Dickerson@verizon.net
To: Nicholls@btinternet.com
Feb. 29, 2007

Dear Stephen

You <u>knew</u> I'd have to look up lapidary.

In class we're reading everyone on my list except Mrs. Gaskell, and as I already told you, Mrs. Gaskell's letters are about Charlotte Bronte, – and we are reading Charlotte Bronte's <u>Jane Eyre</u>. Gross says Mrs. Gaskell is at the top of the second class of Victorian novelists. He says that if we had a little more time for one more novelist to read for the class, it would be her. Gross makes a special case for reading Wilkie Collins, who in his view is also short of the "major" novelist category, but – there's always a but, right? – Collins is terribly important as having written the most famous "sensation" novel, <u>The Woman in White</u>. Gross also says some people wouldn't put Samuel Butler on the A list either. As I mentioned earlier, I never heard of Butler, or Collins either for that matter. And certainly not Mrs. Gaskell. But Gross says Butler is terrific fun when he is blasting away at everything the Victorians stood for and believed in. In any case the Butler novel we're reading in class has a hot title, <u>The Way of All Flesh</u>, but I understand that that title is something of a false lead. But when my gggf was writing his letters to Butler, this was way before <u>The Way of All Flesh</u> was published in 1903, and besides 1903 was actually after Butler's death. Whatever. We're going to read it. Gross says George Bernard Shaw thought it the greatest novel of its time.

Okay, you do the math, as we say over here. I got Dickens, Thackeray, Eliot, Trollope, Hardy, and Butler, six of the top eight, and I only lack the two Bronte sisters because they were dead before my gggf started writing to these novelists. And Mrs. Gaskell writes about both Brontes in her letters to my gggf, so I <u>almost</u> have them too. Then I have Collins and Mrs. Gaskell, tops of the second tier — you might call them numbers nine and ten in the all time Victorian top ten fiction lineup. And I sit there in the class with letters of theirs in my pocket, as they say. Like everybody over here is always saying, it's "mind boggling." And they give "boggling" three syllables, whereas I heard on public radio that the word should be pronounced with only two syllables "bog-gling." At some point I'm probably going to tell Gross about my letters and my project, but for the time being I'm playing it cagey.

Yours
Larry

Gross says that the next two novelists (you could call them number eleven and twelve on the list) are George Gissing and George Meredith. About these two Gross says that Gissing is so depressing as to be "dangerous to your health," and that Meredith is so difficult that he is "the only Victorian novelist who needs to be translated into English." Thank God I can give those two a miss.

Thanks on Bentham. How do you <u>know</u> these things?

From: Nicholls@btinternet.com
To: L.Dickerson@verizon.net
3 March 2007

Dear Larry

Glad to hear your enthusiasm continues unabated. I can see the dilemma: if you tell your instructor about your letters, he will quite naturally want to see the originals, and it would be hard to explain to him – as you have done with me over a period of months – how for the present you don't wish to share the originals with anyone. I do hope you'll be sharing them with me very soon.

You might very well have known the word "lapidary."

Yours lapidarily
Stephen

Bentham. Perhaps you didn't know that at university I read English, which is to say, in American terms, I was an "English major."

From: L.Dickerson@verizon.net
To: Nicholls@btinternet.com
March 4, 2007

Dear Stephen

    My God, I should have known. An English major. Well, there you go, the perfect adviser for me in this business.
    Don't kid me, you knew damn well I would have to look up lapidary, which I did. Nice word. Nice roots, rocks and all that.

You've hit the nail on the head about my dilemma of wanting to ask Gross questions and at the same time bursting with the temptation of telling him after class about my letters but all the while not wanting to show them to him. I'll go cautiously and play it by ear.

Gross handed out lists – "bibliographies" – for each novelist we are doing: editions of letters, biographies, and criticism for each writer. He put great emphasis on the importance of letters. He says that a person's letters are "factual" in a way that other writings about this person, like biographies, aren't. You can imagine the secret thrill that gave me. These published collections of letters – I'm still just learning to call them "editions" – are huge: 12 volumes for Dickens, for example (about 20,000 letters by Dickens exist), and 9 volumes of George Eliot Letters. No chance of buying these books as they are outrageously expensive. The Pilgrim Edition Dickens Letters would cost way over two thousand bucks. I'm heading to the big New York Public Library on Fifth Avenue and 42nd street (not a dinky little branch library like we have here in the Village). It will be exciting to see what letters look like when printed out in an official "edition." You might even say I am coming up with my own little edition of my great-great-grandfather's correspondence ("Edited by Lawrence Dickerson").

As for biographies, I figure I'll "read around" in them so as to pick up something about my novelists around the time my gggf was in touch with them. Sound right to you? There are so many biographies that I asked Gross to tell me which to look into. Dickens, for example, has dozens and dozens of biographies about him – and hundreds of "critical works," which I am ignoring. Gross says that for years the great biography of Dickens was by Edgar Johnson, of New York's own City College, in two volumes, no less. From the 1950s. For years this was the "standard" life. But then another guy, also here at City University of New York, by the name of Kaplan moved in with a pretty impressive large biography – but only one volume, thank God. Then an Englishman by the name of Peter Ackroyd follows up on Kaplan with another one volume life of Dickens, but it's 1100 pages! Gross says their different views on Dickens's 12 year affair with an actress make for a good example of how difficult it is to "visit the past" and to find out what really happened. But the mistress business sounds like hot stuff. Ackroyd believes it was a "romantic" connection but never sexually consummated. Fat chance.

I'm actually going to buy some biographies so I can keep them handy. My plan is to get cheap used copies at the Strand Bookstore. Gross said that whenever out of town English professors come to New York, they always go straight to the Strand Bookstore. It's just around the block from where I live and it advertises 18 miles of books or some ridiculous number like that.

I tell you all this to let you know that I am more immersed than ever in this project. You can see I am up to my ears in reading and transcribing. Trust me to get everything to you as soon as I can.

Yours
Larry

⌒

From: Nicholls@btinternet.com
To: L.Dickerson@verizon.net
/ March 2007

Dear Larry

I'm continually impressed by your energy. And as a dealer in manuscripts, I can certainly agree that old letters written by famous people have a genuine magic to them. This is true of nearly anything someone like Dickens wrote, but if, as you indicate, your letters have real substance to them, these are special objects indeed.

And yes, just "read around" in the biographies for material pertinent to your project. Here's a bit of pedantic advice: <u>Ars longa vita brevis</u>: Art is long, life is short. Stay on your target: the transcriptions.

I've heard people speak of the Strand Bookstore but have, unfortunately, never been there. I've only visited New York twice and for short periods on Christie's business. Next time I'll see the Strand and you.

Best
Stephen

PS The New York Public Library is one of the three or four greatest libraries in the world. Christie's has handled many manuscripts and rare books for the Library over the past century. You are privileged to live right down the street from such a place.

⟨———⟩

From: Dickerson@verizon.net
To: Nicholls@btinternet.com
March 7, 2007

Dear Stephen

    Thanks.
    Thought you'd get a kick out of a little incident in class: one young woman in our course said the books we were reading weren't political enough for her. She said they weren't socially "meaningful." She announced that Great Expectations meant nothing to her because she didn't see any message in it. "What's the point?" she asked Gross. He's a very verbal man but for a moment he was speechless. Then he mumbled something about what was the point of a Mozart violin trio, or something, and then just settled back in amazement. In my day the professor would have chewed her out for asking such a dumb question – what's the point of Great Expectations? He would've said that from now on he would accept only intelligent questions and moved on. If Gross said something like that today, the student would go whining to the dean that she was verbally abused in his class.

Yours
Larry

> 46 <

From: Nicholls@btinternet.com
To: L.Dickerson@verizon.net
8 March 2007

Dear Larry

I did enjoy hearing of the little dustup in your university class. There are often nutty political students, but in my experience they usually get that way because of their professors. Not that students cannot become crazy by themselves, becoming, for example, arch-aesthetes who go around doing little but discerning different shades of purple and reading Walter Pater. Both extremes are usually just phases. Things like this happen at university because, in my view, people out in the world can't afford the time to be so frivolous.

Best
Stephen

From: L.Dickerson@verizon.net
To: Nicholls@btinternet.com
March 8, 2007

Stephen

I don't know Walter Pater and don't want to. When you're dealing with the greatest writers of the century, you can't keep track of all the little fellows.

Larry

From: Nicholls@btinternet.com
To: L.Dickerson@verizon.net
8 March 2007

Fine with me. Keep to your transcriptions. I'm eager to see them.

Stephen

⌒〜

From: L.Dickerson@verizon.net
To: Nicholls@btinternet.com
March 17, 2007

Stephen

I <u>am</u> keeping at them. I know you're eager and I'm doing my best.

Larry

PS You'll be glad to hear that that woman dropped out of class. Such crap – wanting to know what's the point of <u>Great Expectations</u>.
　　Gross says one big division among writers is into putter-inners of words and taker-outers of words. Faulkner being the prime example of a of putter-inner, and Hemingway being the prime example of a taker-outer. The first keeps piling on the words, while the second strives to be "economic" in the use of words. Sounds sensible? On the other hand, what the hell good is a division like this if most writers fall into a middle area? I am sticking to the Victorians. As I just said, when you're dealing with the best novelists of them all you don't have time for the little guys of the next century.

⌒〜

From: Nicholls@btinternet.com
To: L.Dickerson@verizon.net
17 March 2007

Dear Larry

An American student of letters calling Hemingway and Faulkner "little guys." Do not tell that to someone in the Books and Manuscripts department of a major auction house.

Yours, shocked,
Stephen

From: L.Dickerson@verizon.net
To: Nicholls@btinternet.com
March 18, 2007

Dear Stephen

You yourself say life is short and art is long, and at this point in time I don't have time for anyone out of the Victorian period.

I've been spending time at the New York Public Library. After what you said about it, I felt the way a Catholic must when he visits St. Peters, or a Muslim when he gets to Mecca or wherever it is they go. The "Reading Room" is two blocks long with no supporting columns, one of the longest rooms in the world. You fill out a little slip of paper next door in the "Catalog Room" and get a ticket like at a Chinese laundry. Then half an hour later the number on your ticket lights up on a sign and you go up and get the book. You have to read it in the Reading Room. No borrowing of books. That's why they have the books in the first place – it's not so easy to steal or lose them. Maybe you know all this stuff. In any case, so far I have located the twelve volumes of Dickens letters, the six of Thackeray, and the nine of George Eliot and her "husband" Lewes. My God those people wrote letters.

On the negative side, I don't find any of my gggf's letters included in these huge editions of letters. He is never listed in the Index of Correspondents – or even in the General Index. I keep hoping to find him there, but he isn't in any of these collections that I've looked into.

Yours
Larry

From: Nicholls@btinternet.com
To: L.Dickerson@verizon.net
18 March 2007

Dear Larry

Please do not be disheartened. Your letters are not mentioned because neither your great-great-grandfather nor his descendants after him dispersed or sold them, and that's why you have them and also why they are of such considerable interest and value. So you can be happy not to find Jeremy MacDowell there. It makes your collection unique.

Best
Stephen

From: L.Dickerson@verizon.net
To: Nicholls@btinternet.com
March 18, 2007

Dear Stephen

Thanks. What you say makes as per usual good sense.
I notice that these editions give you everything they have for each letter, which includes the printed letterhead. For Dickens it's "Gad's Hill

Place, Higham by Rochester, Kent" – a funny sounding address if you ask me. And for Thackeray "36 Onslow Square, Brompton." I feel right at home reading a letter from Gad's Hill or Onslow Square. What's more, even the big fancy Pilgrim Edition of Dickens Letters can't show – like mine can – the way these letterheads are printed with raised letters and sometimes in color.

   What huge projects publishing all these letters must have been. The Dickens Pilgrim Edition began in the 1950s and ended after 2000. Most of the "founding editors" were dead before the damn thing was completed. And you tell me to hurry, which looks like good advice.

                                        Yours
                                        Larry

PS I'm starting to look at the collected letters of Hardy next week. I see that Hardy lived nearly forever. Here he was, a Victorian novelist who gave up writing novels in 1895 after everybody called Jude the Obscure obscene, and yet he only died in 1928. An easy year for an older American man to remember because it was just one year after Babe Ruth hit his record 60 home runs. Excuse the baseball again, but it's in my blood.

   I picked up a whole shelf of biographies at the Strand. Jesus, there's a lot of information here. I alternate my time between transcribing the letters and reading the novels mentioned in them, and checking biographies and letters for incidents mentioned in my letters. A hell of a big job.

                              ⌒

From: Nicholls@btinternet.com
To: L.Dickerson@verizon.net
20 March 2007

Dear Larry

I'm glad to hear of your industry, but I infer what is obvious, namely, that your wider involvement is going to slow down your transcribing and in turn delay our handling the letters at auction for you. I was about to say, if indeed you ever do auction them. I'm only kidding.

Best
Stephen

⌒

From: L.Dickerson@verizon.net
To: Nicholls@btinternet.com
March 21, 2007

Dear Stephen

Hey, don't you go sounding discouraged about this. Even in kidding.
Of course I mean to auction them and to have you and Christie's do the auctioneering. I can't send you xeroxes yet because I can't let go yet. I want to dig in and learn all there is about the letters and then bring out a self-published paperback book, a little "edition" of all my transcriptions and commentary. In spite of Gross being against self-publishing. This book would come out after you sell the originals at Christie's. What a day that will be. The selling, I mean.

Yours
Larry

Did I ever tell you that when I was in grade school, the school doctor – I don't know if he was a real doctor – told my parents that I was not only an "underachiever" but that I "obsessed" over the little handful of things that did interest me. How did he know? For a time I was obsessed with building model airplanes and then setting them on fire.

⌒

From: Nicholls@btinternet.com
To: L.Dickerson@verizon.net
22 March 2007

Dear Larry

Yes, it will be a big day. We'll have a special catalogue printed and illustrated for the sale. The title will be something like <u>The MacDowell Papers: Letters of Dickens, Thackeray, George Eliot, Mrs Gaskell, Trollope, Collins, Hardy, Butler, and Darwin</u>. This catalogue will incorporate parts of your explanatory commentary.

As for being obsessive, if you are (and I see considerable evidence in that direction), then you should, I think, give in and be obsessive. Consider the fact that all of "your" writers (as you label them) were obsessive workers — Trollope most especially so, but actually every one of them. I think one finds that people who amount to anything in any field are obsessive. So, don't trouble yourself about a diagnosis made decades ago that may indeed be correct. Just keep in the back of your obsessive mind that you are going to deliver all this material to me in due course, or, rather, as soon as possible.

Best
Stephen

From: L.Dickerson@verizon.net
To: Nicholls@btinternet.com
March 23, 2007

Dear Stephen

    Thanks for what I <u>think</u> were kind words on my obsessiveness. In any case, I appreciate your patience about getting the originals, even though I am sensing that your patience is growing thin sometimes. For which I don't blame you.

Yours
Larry

But another thing. What are a few months here in this regard? I will send the originals to you "in due course," as you say. Do you know you use "in due course" a lot? Maybe my in due course is a little late, but what's the difference? For all I know the letters may be going up in value as we speak. And so, maybe the later the better. Unless I should go and croak before I finish.

From: Nicholls@btinternet.com
To: L.Dickerson@verizon.net
25 March 2007

Dear Larry

You must work at your own pace, of course. I was only suggesting you give priority to the actual transcriptions of the letters.

Best
Stephen

From: L.Dickerson@verizon.net
To: Nicholls@btinternet.com
March 26, 2007

Right! Yes, Sir! Sargent Nicholls! The transcriptions get first priority and my commentary takes a back seat. Fair enough. But transcribing is really "editing," as I've learned, and it's not as easy as it sounds. For example, you have to decide whether or not to correct things like spelling – would you believe Trollope always spells George Eliot with two l's? Or whether to leave it and put in "sic" meaning "thus," meaning that the mistake is right there in the original.

Look, I know you are anxious. Suppose I send you in advance some typical transcribed letters, to let you see some typical content. I'm sending you here the second letter Dickens wrote to my gggf – the first as I already explained is rather short. Here goes:

Gad's Hill Place.
Higham by Rochester, Kent

July 30, 1861

Dear Mr. MacDowell,

What you ask is a fair enough question. I know some critics have said that my later books are "darker" than my earlier ones. I think I remain fundamentally optimistic, but I believe that older men, all of them, not just writers, come to know too much and have lost some little of their faith in human beings. On the other hand, I would never apply the word pessimistic to myself. But I am more thoughtful than the young man who dashed off Pickwick twenty-five years ago.

As to the "originals" of my characters, I'll say that frequently one character draws on various real personages; and, what is almost the same thing, that sometimes a character of mine embodies only a touch, a characteristic touch, of an actual human being from the real world. But this is odd of me to contrast the real world and the world of my stories because for me my characters are real. I hear them speak. The world of my mind is as real to me as is the so-called real world outside my mind. People say my characters are "fantastic," but I don't see it that way. They are real. Others say my characters are caricatures. If they are caricatures, I answer that caricatures are as real as actual living persons – sometimes in fact "more real" than actual persons. But I suppose I do have a fondness for peculiarities, for eccentricities – like Mr Micawber's quaint verbal strengths, his changing frame of mind, swaying back and forth between optimistic and pessimistic (but always rounding round to the former). People like him do exist in the world. A writer must keep his eyes and ears open.

My favourite among my works, as I have said publicly, is David Copperfield. I think the reason is the partly self-portrait I put into the chief character. And yes, there is something of yours truly in Pip in Great Expectations, also; but then there is a good deal of the author in every character he creates. They come from him; I said above that they reflect actual persons or more usually peculiar features of those persons; but the characters come onto the page through the writer, so they all bear something of his stamp or his image. One may ask where else could they come from if not from his mind? But I seem close to wrapping myself in circles here, saying that my characters are partial incarnations of actual people, and at the same time insisting they originate in my imagination. Both statements are true.

Still, it's hard to point to favourite novels. It is easier for me to point to favourite episodes or favourite characters. And here, if I may be allowed some immodesty, there is plenty to choose from: scenes like Oliver asking for more, the murder of Nancy by Sikes, the trial in Pickwick; characters like Mrs Gamp, Mr Toots, Bucket the detective, Mr Dick, old Mr Dorrit — I think Mr Dorrit (I say so who should not) is a true "original" except that, as above, such peculiar people do exist in our peculiar world. All this sounds like boasting. Destroy this letter.

Yours truly
ChasDickens

Only about 217 letters to go, counting of course my gggf's letters.

Yours
Larry

From: Nicholls@btinternet.com
To: L.Dickerson@verizon.net
28 March 2007

Dear Larry

The Dickens letter you sent almost made me lose my English reserve.
People in my line of work are supposed to be coolly distanced. If the
other letters are anywhere near as meaty as this one, you are sitting on
shockingly important letters.

Best
Stephen

Chapter Five

From: L.Dickerson@verizon.net
To: Nicholls@btinternet.com
April 2, 2007

Dear Stephen

Glad you liked the Dickens letter.

Brace yourself for a New Jersey vulgarism of my youth: the sunshine is coming out of my ass today. Here's the story. I have a niece, Ellen, who lives in Cranford in New Jersey. Way back when, when they were breaking up the house after my mother died, I got this box of old letters and some pictures, and my older brother Joey, now deceased, got all the books. His daughter Ellen some time back had a secondhand book dealer come to her house. He picked out the books he wanted and gave her about $3700. My feeling is this guy must have picked out the cream – Dickens et al – and left her with a lot of junk by people no one ever heard of anymore.

Anyhow, I told her about my project – not giving the whole thing away, of course. I have to play my cards close to the vest even with my own niece because these letters may prove to be a gold mine, as you well know. But, in any case, after I told her what I was doing, she told me that among the crummy stuff that the book dealer couldn't be bothered with was an old notebook with handwriting in it. She said it was probably Jeremy MacDowell's handwriting – and she'd be happy to send it to me.

Well, yesterday this brown paper package arrives from Cranford. When I opened it and looked at the notebook, my heart started beating like a captured robin. For one thing, it is definitely in my gggf's handwriting. If I know anybody's handwriting, I know his. (Although I find it funny that many of my authors have almost the same handwriting – as if they all went to the same school.)

On the front of this notebook is a pasted label on which my gggf has written "Reading." This notebook is a running list of all the books he read from 1859 up almost until his death. For each book he gives a date when he finished reading it (we know he was a great one for dates). And for certain books he writes in comments. Some comments are long and some very short, like "Boring stuff" or "Not worth the time." What a reader he must have been. Of course he was in the book business. The very first book mentioned in the notebook is On Liberty by J. S. Mill, and my gggf finished it on November 29, 1859. He gives this very brief comment on it: "A convincing, carefully argued, remarkable book." I never heard of Mill except for you calling him a saint once.

I've had only a quick look through this notebook, which is about the size of an account ledger. Whadyathink?

Yours
Larry

PS I can't help thinking that that book dealer took Ellen to the cleaners half a dozen years ago. Probably did very well for himself. But that's water over the dam. Of course Ellen was glad to get that much. Too bad she didn't ship them all over to you. I bet he robbed her blind. She didn't know anything about books, and neither did I, then. But my gggf must have had plenty of old books worth a lot more money than what he gave her.

From: Nicholls@btinternet.com
To: L.Dickerson@verizon.net
3 April 2007

Dear Larry

That is exciting about Jeremy MacDowell's reading record. Just so much more context for your letters. This is a stroke of good fortune.

Let me know of any other surprises. In fact, you seem to possess now what in the business is called an "archive" of your great-great-grandfather's manuscript letters and other pertinent materials.

Yours
Stephen

To return to some points in your last email: John Stuart Mill was a famous free thinker and philosopher. And <u>On Liberty</u> is considered the finest expression of political liberalism. Mill once went into Parliament, friends having prevailed upon him to do so, and while a member of Parliament he put forth an amendment (substituting the word "person" for "man" in a voting bill) that would have given the vote to women. It was defeated, of course, and women had to wait sixty years to gain the right to vote in the UK. Mill also said, famously, that the conservative party was "the stupidest Party." He didn't say, he explained, that all conservatives were stupid, just that stupid people were generally conservative, and that the conservative party had to have a large number of, or a constituency of, stupid people voting with them, people uninformed enough to think that the conservative party supported their interests, when in fact conservative policies generally favour the upper classes and the financially well off. Rather like poor people in your country thinking they should be Republicans. Or, in this country, thinking they should be Tories. Excuse my going on.

It's possible the book dealer acted somewhat high-handedly with your niece; on the other hand, in my experience most antiquarian book dealers are honest people. (And remember Jeremy MacDowell himself was a bookseller.) Of course book dealers can't pay anything like the retail value of a book; they live on the markup, which is generally about 70%.

⁓

From: L.Dickerson@verizon.net
To: Nicholls@btinternet.com
April 4, 2007

Dear Stephen

     Yeah this notebook certainly is a piece of very good luck. Talk about context. I'm as happy as a pig in s---, as we used to say. You can imagine my excitement as I started to look for entries that connect to "my" letters. What I have to do, of course, is read slowly and carefully from one end to the other of this notebook and see where it intersects with letters to Dickens, Thackeray and so on. (You have me so nervous about "etc" that I avoid it as much as possible.) It's a lot of work, coordinating and so on. But I am going at it full tilt. I have found a second life, you might say. Other old birds if they don't have anything to do just sit around feeling sorry for themselves and then die off quickly. I'm throwing myself into this project like mad. Just to give you a taste of what is in the "Reading" notebook, I can tell you that my eye came across some lines of his about Tess of the D'Urbervilles and "the ache of modernism" – which I must check out. This ache of modernism is one of the very things my gggf wrote to Hardy about. How's that for a connection?

                                        Yours
                                        Larry

PS   70% sounds pretty steep.

⁓

From: Nicholls@btinternet.com
To: L.Dickerson@verizon.net
6 April 2007

Dear Larry

You mentioned inheriting pictures when the letters came into your possession. Can you tell me what they are? It's just possible they may be worth something.

Best
Stephen

PS   70% is not steep. You try to sell an old book sometime and you'll see. To begin with, you wouldn't know how to get customers. That's what used and rare book dealers do, they provide a place where customers have access to books, even if only over the phone, or nowadays on the Internet. And they have to keep an office, pay rent, hire employees, pay utility bills, etc, all the while sitting on stock (books) that sometimes doesn't move for years. I grant you the Web is changing secondhand book selling, but the markup is always high. A book by some completely unheard of Victorian novelist (and there are literally thousands of such novels) is very "scarce" and indeed "rare," but the problem is that if no one wants to buy it, the book is worthless. Demand, or "call," is everything. A book may be 200 years old – or 300 years old – and have no value. And recent, or practically new books, even in mint condition, are worth very little. You pay £20 for a new book and take it around the corner to a used book dealer, and you'll be lucky to get a pound, or in your case two dollars.

From: L.Dickerson@verizon.net
To: Nicholls@btinternet.com
April 6, 2007

Dear Stephen

As regards the pictures, my wife, who died seven years ago, got rid of them. There was nothing good, just stuff in black and white, prints as we say. Nothing at all in color. But it certainly is fortuitous that we kept the box with the letters.

Yours
Larry

I take your word for it on the business of buying and selling books. You know what you are talking about, and I am of course a rookie here. In any case I'll forget the books – they're gone anyway – and concentrate on my manuscripts, my "ALSs," as you call them.

From: Nicholls@btinternet.com
To: L.Dickerson@verizon.net
6 April 2007

I can't keep myself from asking why you are using "fortuitous" here. It's a word I confess to being very sensitive and even snobbish about. It means "by chance" – nothing to do with good chance, or good luck, as we say. Sorry for being pedantic.

From: L.Dickerson@verizon.net
To: Nicholls@btinternet.com
April 7, 2007

Why don't you just come out and say you think I used the wrong word? But over here in America "fortuitous" seems to mean lucky and good. I remember during the last Super Bowl – that's football – I heard the TV announcer say the ball took a fortuitous bounce – meaning a nice lucky bounce – into the player's hands. Now if that isn't convincing, what is? On the television, no less, with millions of people watching?

From: Nicholls@btinternet.com
To: L.Dickerson@verizon.net
7 April 2007

Far be it from me to argue with a TV sports announcer. I take your word for how the word is used in America. We live and learn. You know of course that in the UK and in the rest of the world, "football" is what you call "soccer." And, on the subject of words, here's something that will give you a bit of an advantage over your sports-loving friends: tell them that the word "soccer" comes from "association" – "association football" – as the game was once called here in England, the country of its birth.

From: L.Dickerson@verizon.net
To: Nicholls@btinternet.com
April 8, 2007

Dear Stephen

Nice bit of news about the word "soccer." It's good to hear you talk about something out of your field of specialty. Go ahead, enlighten me on some other sports word.

Yours
Larry

⌐⌐⌐

From: Nicholls@btinternet.com
To: L.Dickerson@verizon.net
8 April 2007

Dear Larry

Just because I work in a somewhat rarefied "field" doesn't mean I don't care about – well – football, for example. Sports words? I did read that for you Americans to call the big baseball playoff "the World Series" doesn't mean you are claiming to be the summit of everything in the world; rather, according to a letter to the editor of the TLS, the name "World Series" derives from a long-defunct New York newspaper called The World, which originally sponsored the games.

Best
Stephen

⌐⌐⌐

From: L.Dickerson@verizon.net
To: Nicholls@btinternet.com
April 8, 2007

Stephen

Damn. I hope you are right about the World Series because there I really would have something on my buddies. They would never know that, and they'd be impressed – whether it was true or not, actually. I would love to talk sports with you but I have a feeling you are just humoring me because you know that all Americans, all the men that is – and boys too – are crazy nuts about sports. One after the other, baseball season, then football, then basketball. I don't follow hockey because I figure three is enough. But in England you have only one real sport – not counting things like track and swimming which don't really count as major – and that's why everybody there is hooked on soccer.

Larry

⌒

From: Nicholls@btinternet.com
To: L.Dickerson@verizon.net
9 April 2007

We do play tennis.

⌒

From: L.Dickerson@verizon.net
To: Nicholls@btinternet.com
April 9, 2007

You play tennis but you don't win. When was the last time you won anything at Wimbledon? Must be a hundred years ago. I'm not counting girls tennis where you may have won once way back thirty or forty years ago.

⌒

From: Nicholls@btinternet.com
To: L.Dickerson@verizon.net
10 April 2007

Larry

We must "count" the women. Virginia Wade won in 1977. Fred Perry won three times back in the 1930s. I'll grant you that that was a long time ago.

Stephen

Chapter Six

From: L.Dickerson@verizon.net
To: Nicholls@btinternet.com
April 13, 2007

Dear Stephen

Okay. I'm settling down to my Dickens stuff. I told you that in our class Gross is stressing the biographies of our writers and looking for "echoes" of the same stuff in their novels. In Dickens's case, he wants us to look at certain women in the novels, like Dora the "child wife" he kills off in <u>David Copperfield</u>, and Estella, the big sexual tease in <u>Great Expectations</u>. He thinks Charles Dickens (that is, David Copperfield) in the 1840s is already getting tired of Catherine, his own "child wife." And he thinks Estella may owe a lot to Ellen Ternan. Here the real point is that people believe what they want to believe. Certain true "Dickensians," most of them old enough to know better, won't believe that for 12 years he had a mistress. For them Dickens is a combination of Shakespeare and Jesus. They only admit he was "obsessed" – like me with these letters – with this young woman (young when they started – she was 18 and he was 45, and it lasted till his death 12 or 13 years later). The object of his affections was a young actress named Ellen Ternan. She was exactly the age of Dickens's <u>third</u> oldest child, Kate. One old friend of Dickens said she had "a voluptuous figure." We know what that means, but since you are English I'm not going to use regular straight American words here. He meets her at a play he was producing and then he has a big midlife crisis. He separates from his wife – they had been married 20 years and had 10 children. Dickens keeps all the kids but one with himself.

Then he stupidly publishes a letter in the newspapers saying that his wife Catherine had a mental disorder and that she had been asking for a separation for years, and that "certain wicked persons" had spread "abominable" rumors about a young woman and him. You can imagine how many people believed him. Probably only Dickens himself.

In any case, for a dozen years Dickens, like a character in one of his novels, lives a double life, and he does a very good job of hiding what was going on. He plies her (and her mother and sisters) with money and gifts, and makes it possible for her to retire from the stage (actresses were suspect). He rents various houses for her in the suburbs under a disguised name, "Charles Tringham." He manages to get away with it for the most part, though during these twelve years the rumor never completely died. But the people who knew about it, including for sure Trollope's brother Tom, kept quiet, or at least they never wrote it down. The whole business really only came out in the 1930s. Around then, Dickens's son Henry and his daughter Kate separately told friends about it, and these friends went public after Henry and Kate were dead. So technically this evidence was "hearsay" even though it was coming from his own children. Henry even said, "There was a child, but it died." But after that, all sorts of evidence came out. There was even some disputed testimony that Dickens did not die at his home at Gad's Hill, but at Ellen's place and that Ellen managed to get the body home in a cab in time for his sister-in-law to set the scene to make it look like he died there. Reminds me of the death of Nelson Rockefeller.

Still, like I said, many important Dickens scholars (like that Peter Ackroyd in his 1100 page book) won't admit the affair was "consummated." It's like you or me trying to believe that some particular married couple who never had any children never had any sex because no one was there to witness it and take pictures. These fanatical Dickensians won't admit that their great man could have a mistress. For them he was the "inventor" of Christmas and also the great "bulwark of the family." It sounds like our "family values" crap. These fanatics can't believe he was an ordinary adulterer like so many other men. I was about to say like the rest of us.

Yours
Larry

Here's my very first "attachment" – a fuzzy old photograph of Ellen Ternan taken around the time when she met Dickens and when she was 18. Tell me if it comes through.

From: Nicholls@btinternet.com
To: L.Dickerson@verizon.net
14 April 2007

Dear Larry

That striking photograph picture came through just fine. I knew something of the affaire Dickens. But you are becoming a regular adept at searching out the stories of "your" novelists.

What about Jeremy MacDowell's letters to and from Dickens?

Best
Stephen

From: L.Dickerson@verizon.net
To: Nicholls@btinternet.com
April 15, 2007 (Income tax day here)

Dear Stephen

Okay. For one thing, my gggf couldn't come right out and ask, "So how're you and your actress doing?" But you can't tell me he wasn't thinking of the mistress vs. the wife when he asked CD about "originals" for his characters as per the first letter I sent you. But still, my gggf had to be careful to stick to the literary side. For example he tells Dickens that he thinks the chapter called "Podsnappery" in Our Mutual Friend is the best thing ever written on the English being anti-foreigner. And this was from a guy who adored Thackeray who, I understand, was always making fun of the English being so English and so superior to foreigners, especially the French. In any case I went right to that Podsnap chapter in Our Mutual Friend, and I can say my gggf was "spot on" as you say in England. If you haven't read it since you were in school or in college, you should read it now that you are grown up. Nothing like it. This rich fellow John Podsnap is completely satisfied with himself and with England and he wonders why everyone else isn't satisfied, too. He thinks that foreign countries are in general "a mistake." Their biggest mistake is that they are "Not English." Dickens has a lot of fun with that and with another key point in Podsnappery. And this is to condemn anything that might come close to "bringing a blush to the cheek of the young person." This of course is a way of saying that anything to do with sex was off limits to young English women. You'd think they had to wonder where babies came from – probably from kissing or something like that. But Dickens's attack on sexual prudery is coming from a man with a long-standing mistress. You see the connection?

Dickens thanks my gggf for his praise, but you get the feeling that he, Dickens, felt that this kind of raving about a single chapter might just imply a little putting down of the rest of Our Mutual Friend. So I'd say that Dickens's thank you is a bit unenthusiastic. But you'll judge for yourself when I send you "in due course" all the transcriptions.

Yours
Larry

⌢

From: Nicholls@btinternet.com
To: L.Dickerson@verizon.net
16 April 2007

Dear Larry

I had to read <u>Our Mutual Friend</u> while preparing for A levels (like your SATs) but can't remember much of it. But I did know the word "podsnappery." You will find it is in the dictionary.

Best
Stephen

⌢

From: L.Dickerson@verizon.net
To: Nicholls@btinternet.com
April 17, 2007

Dear Stephen

I take your word for the word being in your dictionary. Although it isn't in either of my "college" size dictionaries. One of these is the <u>American Heritage Dictionary</u> and maybe that dictionary is too American to bother with a word that has to do with being too English. You'd think though that the word would be in my other dictionary, <u>The New World Dictionary</u>. It isn't. But I checked in the big <u>Webster's Unabridged Dictionary</u> – the one they keep on the stand in the library

– and of course it's in there. You figure if that dictionary is "unabridged" and if "podsnappery" is really a word, then it would <u>have</u> to be in there, right?

Yours
Larry

Did I tell you that my gggf was always asking his novelists what they thought of illustrations in novels? I didn't think it was an important question and figured it could wait till you got everything. But now a sneaking suspicion tells me that it may be an important thing after all. Because I have learned that so many of "my" novelists' novels first appeared in magazines and almost all magazines had illustrations. I know that today if you buy a novel by a famous person, John Updike or Philip Roth or that Shirley Hazzard, it's not at all illustrated. Not even the dust jackets are illustrated, really. And I find that my gggf was very much against illustrated novels – except for Dickens and Thackeray. For example, in a "reading" note after finishing Hardy's <u>Tess</u>, he says, "The book version is incomparably superior to the illustrated version as serialised monthly in the Graphic. The pictures are a blot on the book. Thank God they were not carried over to the book edition."

⌒

From: Nicholls@btinternet.com
To: L.Dickerson@verizon.net
18 April 2007

Dear Larry

In fact, illustrated fiction is a subject that interests me immensely. I used to work in Prints and Drawings. Besides, our department handles many illustrated books. Tell me more of what your letters say.

Best
Stephen

From: L.Dickerson@verizon.net
To: Nicholls@btinternet.com
April 18, 2007

Dear Stephen

OK. In 1865 Dickens says this to my gggf:

> You ask about illustrators. Publishers arranged for George
> Cruikshank to do my Sketches and Oliver Twist. To this day, his
> drawings for Oliver Twist are my favourites — and everybody else's
> too from what I can tell. I think the illustration of Oliver Asking for
> More deserves the enduring favour it seems to enjoy. I myself hired
> H. K. Browne ("Phiz") for Pickwick, and he was with me for about ten
> novels, for which he produced some marvelous work. I really think
> that he was often unfavourably compared to the eminent
> Cruikshank. But at least Browne tried faithfully to follow my writing
> and my instructions to him. And, in fact, Browne could do some
> sombre scenes for me (as in Bleak House and Little Dorrit) that
> would have been — in my opinion — beyond Cruikshank's powers. In
> spite of what I have just said, I think Browne was at his best in comic
> scenes. His very best work was probably for David Copperfield. See,
> for example, any of those depicting Mr. Micawber. But toward the
> end of my collaboration with Browne, my writing and his drawings
> sometimes did not fit together so well as earlier.

I of course never heard of either George Cruikshank or Hablot
Knight Browne. What the hell kind of a first name is Hablot with a
French looking ^ over the o? And so far I haven't seen any of their
drawings. Go ahead, enlighten me on this business. What do you think
of my gggf thinking that the illustration of novels is usually a mistake?
Hasn't history proved him right?

Yours
Larry

> 74 ‹

From: Nicholls@btinternet.com
To: L.Dickerson@verizon.net
19 April 2007

Dear Larry

This is a subject so dear to me that I run the risk of boring you to tears. And, yes, we today don't want our novels illustrated. Henry James's words on the subject have become famous: he said in effect that, for him, when a novel could be read in either illustrated or unillustrated version, he found it a positive comfort to be left alone with the text. James claimed he realised everything that (under certain conditions) pictures could do for a text and everything that the text could do for the pictures. Still, he went on to confess a jealousy of any "pictorial aid" to fiction coming from "the outside"; fiction is a form which, he insists, can "get on by itself." So, whenever someone tells me he can't stand any illustration to any adult fiction, I accept that there's no sense in arguing with him, or her.

On the other hand, some Victorian novelists, most particularly Dickens, lend themselves wonderfully to illustration. (Of course even in the case of Dickens, there are innumerable passages that simply cannot be illustrated. I'll try to paraphrase for you one such description, from A Christmas Carol, where Dickens writes that Scrooge's house was a gloomy suite of rooms in a pile of buildings up a yard, a place where it had so little business being that you could scarcely keep from fancying that as a young house it must have run into that yard, playing hide-and-seek with other houses, got lost, and forgotten its way out again. Something to that effect. It's an example of Dickens's famous "animism," the way he could breathe human life into inanimate objects – here a house. No artist who ever lived could depict that house. Every line drawn would have detracted from Dickens's words.)

Excuse that long parenthesis. I'm too brimming with opinions here. I was saying that there was a certain short period when English illustrated fiction flourished quite magically. It began with Dickens's Sketches by Boz, Pickwick, and Oliver Twist in the late 1830s and lasted only until about 1870, with Millais's last drawings for Trollope. Cruikshank's work for Dickens (Sketches and Oliver Twist) and Browne's (Pickwick and the following ten novels) – uneven as it is, dated as some of it is, inept as some of it is – nonetheless at its best complements the novels so well that it does more than "illustrate": it heightens, epitomises, enriches the prose; it doesn't even seem subsidiary or secondary. Opponents of illustrated fiction say it's a hybrid art, but so are opera and ballet, and nobody seems to mind. With the drawings the books are different books; and many of us think better books (though, of course, this is a subjective judgment). I can't imagine anyone wanting Oliver Twist or David Copperfield to be without the Cruikshank and Browne illustrations, respectively.

Cruikshank and Browne were "old school" English graphic satirists, with roots going back to William Hogarth. Their drawing was not just satiric, but lively, imaginative, animated, fairy-tale-like, exaggerated, and often sublimely comic (and, yes, also melodramatic and sentimental). They were, in the very best sense of the word, caricaturists. Their work suited Dickens perfectly; they shared his "realer than real" view of the world.

We all know the old saw about one picture being worth many words, so I send you herewith two images of the drawings your Dickens letter mentions. Here's Cruikshank's drawing of Oliver Asking for More. This drawing from Oliver Twist, Dickens's second novel, has been reproduced so often that it has become emblematic of Dickens. It shows young Oliver, an orphaned (and starving) boy in the refectory of the parish workhouse – poor house – asking for more of the evening gruel. This outlandish request astounds and infuriates the master and Beadle, a fat and "choleric" sadist, who promptly swats Oliver with his ladle, has him put into solitary confinement, flogs him in public regularly, and manages to apprentice (sell) this vile offender of decency to an undertaker. (I know a great deal of this almost by heart because a few years ago I published an article on illustrations to novels in a collection on the Victorian Book.) I remember quoting a prominent critic, J Hillis

Miller, on Cruikshank illustrations for Dickens saying (I paraphrase of course), that the relation between the text and illustration is "reciprocal" in that each refers to the other and illustrates the other, in a back and forth movement, a movement incarnated as the eyes move from text to illustration and back to text again. Accordingly, illustrations "short circuit" the apparent reference in the text to some real world outside. This reciprocal relation of text to illustration sets up "an oscilation" or "shimmering" of meaning, in which neither element is "prior": the pictures are about the text; the test is about the pictures. Some readers of course don't want their mental pictures of starving little Oliver or the fat master "short circuited" by illustrations. Other readers, myself included, believe that if Dickens guided and approved (as he did) the illiustrations, then they are part of the text. These illustrations have also been praised for providing historical social detail and pointing to places where Dickens wanted the stress to fall. Even Henry James said – admittedly he was speaking of himself as a youngster – that "Oliver Twist seemed more Cruikshank's than Dickens's." Here's the drawing – from a surprisingly weak electronic reproduction. Sorry.

Here's a Browne (Phiz) plate from <u>David Copperfield</u>, Mr Micawber and his family entertaining David and his friend Traddles. Micawber (based partly on Dickens's father) is doing what he likes best, speechifying.

I'll stop now or you'll be sorry you asked.

Best
Stephen

From: L.Dickerson@verizon.net
To: Nicholls@btinternet.com
April 19, 2007

Dear Stephen

A really long email. Nice going.
I like the Cruikshank best. He's got strange faces on the boys – not at all realistic, but you can't stop looking at the drawing.

Larry

Chapter Seven

From: L.Dickerson@verizon.net
To: Nicholls@btinternet.com
April 22, 2007

Dear Stephen

I'm skipping ahead to Trollope. Bloody Trollope – see how English I'm becoming? Since I got started on him I'm becoming addicted. Can't read enough of him. And of course as you know there is plenty of him, 47 novels, so you can keep feeding your addiction. Compare this 47 novels as opposed to 15 for Dickens, 8 for Thackeray, 7 for George Eliot, 4 for Charlotte Bronte, etc. If you get into the habit of reading Trollope, you can just keep going. By the time you got to number 47 and started around again at number one, you would have forgotten it, and it would be almost as new as ever.

Now for my Trollope letters. First of all, let me say that Thackeray, in one of his letters, just before he died in 1863, has this to say to my gggf about Trollope. Gross, by the way, says Thackeray is the best letter writer of all the Victorians. He says Thackeray can't send a note turning down a dinner invitation without saying something clever. You can imagine how I wanted to tell him that I had 16 Thackeray letters in a box at home. Gross also says, and this Gross is never at a loss for a strong opinion on anything, that Byron is the best letter writer in all of English. How should I know if he is right? By "best" I think he means smart, clever – you know – charming. In any event here's my Thackeray letter to my gggf on Trollope:

October 11, 1863

My dear MacDowell

 As I think I told you once upon a time about a year ago, Trollope's
<u>Framley Parsonage</u> was much more popular with readers of the
<u>Cornhill Magazine</u> than I was with <u>Lovel the Widower</u>. Now Trollope
himself would have none of this, for he is a positively inordinate
admirer of my fiction, though in his typical manner very critical and
very blunt about what he considers my many shortcomings. He says
that <u>Barry Lyndon</u> is better than <u>Vanity Fair</u> (he is the only mortal I
know who is of this opinion), that Colonel Newcome is my best
character creation (I myself have a warm feeling for the old soldier),
and that <u>Esmond</u> is hands down my best book. This last is
wrong-headed for certain. But Trollope awards the palm to <u>Esmond</u>
because, he avers, I "worked harder" at it, used more of what he
clumsily calls the "elbow grease of the mind" in that novel. He's right
about my working hard at the book, but he's wrong in his lavish
praise of it. He's often wrong, but in a kind of boyish way that once
you catch on to it is almost endearing. He sometimes argues a point
he no more than half believes in himself as if his life depended on it,
and as if yours depended on it as well. He's a prodigious enthusiast
and shouter, and when he's really going at it you have to stand back
for fear of getting hit by the flying bodies of his opponents. Wilkie
Collins says, "He blows my hat off, he turns my umbrella inside out."
Ye gods in heaven, I wonder what he's like in the Post Office. Your
humble servant once foolishly aspired to be Secretary, no less, of the
Post Office, and Trollope with his usual candour tells me it would
have been the end of me in every way had I got the appointment;
that I would have made a terrible muddle of the Post Office and lost
my ability to write into the bargain. He himself is right now charged
with running nearly half of the Post Office of England. And he does it
thoroughly while getting up withal every morning at five and writing
a couple of thousand words on his latest novel. Then, after three

hours' writing, he has breakfast, turns up fresh as paint at the Post Office and works fanatically at his "chief occupation" – getting letters to go where they're supposed to go. And in season he <u>hunts</u> every day. He's not altogether human.

He must be a terrible taskmaster to those slow moving folk under him at the Post Office. He told me once how at a meeting of Surveyors – the heads of the nine postal districts in the Kingdom, he being Surveyor of the Eastern District of England – he announced to them, "I disagree with everything you said," but then had to ask, "What did you say?"

In all departments of life (he also manages to play whist every night at the Garrick Club and to spend an hour a day reading – oh my! – the Latin classics), Trollope evidences prodigious staying power. Of his writings since <u>The Warden</u> and <u>Barchester Towers</u> I've read most of what he has done – nobody could read everything; he's a veritable locomotive. One book is practically as good as the next – and that's saying much. You take, for example, his <u>The Small House at Allington</u>, which is appearing for us in the <u>Cornhill Magazine</u> (where, by the bye, George Smith the publisher does all the work; I was only his figurehead as editor those first two years). <u>The Small House</u> is a fine novel. There's hardly any plot, you might say, but O, mon Dieu, the reality of it; you keep coming back to it as you do to <u>The Times</u> newspaper every morning. He's become enormously popular. Well, says I, may he prosper. He and I have become good friends – in spite of the loudness. I fear he's already losing some of his hearing. Maybe that loud voice has permanently damaged his own ears. In any case, late at night, over cigars and port, he turns down the volume and you find that he is a gentle, sensitive companion, as soft as a girl. That's how he can write those novels. The belligerent, unhelpful arguer and shouter of daylight hours could never write those calm, gentle novels.

You asked about me and I'm talking about Trollope. Writers are often secretive or worse about their working habits. Except for Trollope. He tells you even if you don't ask, about early rising, keeping his watch before him so as to manage 250 words every 15 minutes, etc. Ask him. For my money he's the man to watch in fiction. He churns out two or three books a year (the very thought prostrates me). Mrs. Gaskell, one of our <u>Cornhill</u> contributors, said to George Smith and me that she wished Mr. Trollope "would go on writing <u>Framley Parsonage</u> for ever." That's just what he's doing.

As for myself, I have made an effort to regain something of my public with <u>Philip</u> and my latest, a new opus I'm slaving over in order to put mutton on the table. But if I don't win folks over, I hope readers such as yourself will go back occasionally and take a stroll through the lanes and streets and boulevards of Vanity Fair. It is, though modesty ought to preclude my saying so, a fascinating enough place, for all its humbug.

Your obedient servant etc.
WMThackeray

How's <u>that</u> for an endorsement? After that you don't need me to be telling you how good Trollope is. Incidentally, I am — as "editor" — adding underlinings of titles from here on, even though they are not usually in the original letters.

But I suppose you'd like to see a letter by Trollope himself. Okay. My gggf writes to Trollope telling him that about a year before Thackeray died, he, my gggf, had some nice long letters from Thackeray and that Thackeray spoke very highly of Trollope and his books (as for example in the above letter). That was of course a smart way to cotton up to Trollope because he loved Thackeray. Here's part of my gggf's letter:

We were all distressed by Thackeray's death, even Dickens, with whom he had been quarreling or at least not on speaking terms for years. I understand that a month or so before Thackeray died, he ran into Dickens on the steps of the Club and they shook hands and said, yes, this estrangement must stop. Dickens was at the funeral. I suspect that outside his immediate family, you took his death harder than most. I think it a great idea that you are pushing, viz, having a statue of him made for the Garrick. I doubt the place will be the same without him.

Of course there will be the inevitable comparison both now and *in posterity as to which of these two, Thackeray or Dickens, is the greater novelist. I know what your answer will be, but should like nonetheless to hear it from you.*

Yours sincerely,
Jeremy MacDowell

To this, Trollope replies with this letter:

Waltham House
Waltham Cross

1 March 64

My dear MacDowell,

You're right. Thackeray by a long chalk. Indeed I place Dickens not second but third. George Elliot gets my nod for second place after Thackeray. I used to think Pride and Prejudice *the greatest novel in the language, but then* Henry Esmond *took the crown. I know this is an odd choice from the vast store of Thackeray's writings, but that's what I hold. I believe* Vanity Fair *for all its excellences shows signs of rush and carelessness, whereas* Esmond *is polished, and, to my mind, very nearly perfect. I realise I am going contra mundum here, the public at large favouring* Vanity Fair. *Only time, which of course we don't have, will tell. But at any rate Thackeray is my choice for the foremost English novelist of my day – or any day.*

Of course I admit that no novel is perfection itself – not even any of Thackeray's. Have you ever heard that definition of a novel as a long piece of prose fiction that has something wrong with it? Now, and I am speaking strictly of my own tastes, I prefer simple straightforward writing – ars celare artem – and I don't think Thackeray was of this mind. Dickens and some others, especially Carlyle, write in so idiosyncratic, peculiar, attention-drawing a manner that you are not reading prose, you are reading Dickens, you are reading Carlyle. Gibbon is another such. (Perhaps Swift came closest to writing English, not writing Swift.) Sometimes Thackeray displayed this tendency too, writing Thackeray and not plain English. Still, his writing is absolutely pellucid, and you know without any labour just what he means. More basically, Thackeray knew human nature, and his characters are above all human beings. Indeed our fiction contains no more human characters than his best.

Yours always
Anthony Trollope

As I may have told you Trollope actually spells George Eliot with two "l"s. I guess when you write that much you can't be bothered thinking about spelling.

Yours
Larry

"Pellucid" means "very lucid." Talk about a five dollar word. Ars celare artem? Looks like Latin?

⌒

From: Nicholls@btinternet.com
To: L.Dickerson@verizon.net
23 April (Shakespeare's birthday and deathday) 2007

Dear Larry

Very impressive letters, both the Thackeray and the Trollope.

Best
Stephen

Yes, it's Latin for "Art is to conceal art."

⌒

From: L.Dickerson@verizon.net
To: Nicholls@btinternet.com
April 24, 2007

Dear Stephen

Thanks. But how about my great-great-grandfather's letter? I think it's really amazing how careful he could be in dealing with his correspondents. Writers, and I can believe it, are supposed to be touchy people. And very touchy about their stories and novels. My gggf gets Trollope to talk quite openly about his feelings for his own novels. Trollope says in one of his later letters to my gggf that when people ask him about an old novel of his, like Barchester Towers, he has to say that he "can't remember much of it, because this is what they expect me to say, and it sounds humble." But, Trollope goes on to my gggf, "It ain't so. I remember every word of Barchester Towers." (And sic on "ain't.") Trollope says this in a letter dated August 1880 — that's two years before he died and about 25 years after he wrote Barchester Towers. How's that for getting a famous writer to open up?

My great-great-grandfather also got Trollope to say something about whether Melmotte, the heavy villain of The Way We Live Now, was supposed to be Jewish. Melmotte's wife is Jewish. And everybody in the story thinks he is Jewish. But then towards the very end we read that it turns out that Melmotte was actually an Irishman brought up in New York. This comes as a surprise. And damned if my gggf doesn't put it straight to Trollope, and the old boy comes out and admits that as he was writing the story he was making Melmotte Jewish but then as it came along he changed his mind, because he thought Jews were getting a bad rap and because he, Trollope, "always found Jews more liberal than other people." I think that by liberal here he doesn't mean political liberal, but liberal with money — not cheap. He does, he admits, have a dislike for Jewish money lenders, but everybody disliked money lenders. You could, like him, end up in no time owing the money lender 200 pounds on a 10 pound loan. I'm told the Jews were the money lenders because in the Middle Ages Christians were not allowed to be money lenders. Getting interest on money was a sin — "usury." Who knows? Maybe money lending was just a line of work that Jews were in and stayed in. Like Italian barbers over here, or Irish saloon keepers.

In another later letter, my gggf asked Trollope about what he thought was his greatest novel. This was a big question because there are so many to choose from. In Trollope's time people couldn't even keep count, and some critics complained that he was not taking enough time with his novels. You'll see when I send the transcriptions that Trollope thought the The Last Chronicle of Barset was his best novel. On the other hand, he says he is more interested – like Dickens – in singling out his most successful characters rather than his most successful novels. He names a character from this Last Chronicle, Josiah Crawley, and the two Pallisers, Lady Glencora and Plantagenet Palliser – talk about silly names. "If people read me in the next century," Trollope tells my gggf, "it will be because of these three characters." Now Crawley is based on Trollope's father. That's the hidden autobiographical angle.

OK. Now here's what I can tell you're waiting for:

> Waltham House,
> Waltham Cross

20 May 1864

Dear MacDowell

You ask what I think of Thackeray's illustrations, especially of your favourite book, Vanity Fair. You know that Thackeray as a young man wanted to be an artist. But he never worked hard at it and probably could never have become a successful artist even if he did work at it. You could go so far as to say he never learned to draw. But by drawing – or by not drawing – he made splendid illustrations. Look at Vanity Fair and I think you will agree with me that the delineations are incorrect. On the other hand, his drawings perfectly illustrate the particular passage, by which I mean they perfectly understand the purpose which the writer had in mind in a particular passage. And in some of his adorned capital letters at the

beginnings of chapters he nicely sums up the entire chapter. Of
course the fact that in <u>Vanity Fair</u> *writer and illustrator were the*
same man accounts for much in this regard; but I do think Thackeray
was a marvelous illustrator — though as I said, not much of an artist.

Yours always
Anthony Trollope

Myself, I didn't even know that <u>Vanity Fair</u> was illustrated. I haven't even looked at the book yet because Gross is saving it till near the end of his course.

Yours
Larry

Thanks on Shakespeare. Trollope was born on April 24 — today.

From: Nicholls@btinternet.com
To: L.Dickerson@verizon.net
25 April 2007

Dear Larry

Thanks on Trollope's birthday. I certainly did not know that.

Indeed, if you count not only the forty full-page plates but the many small in-text drawings and the capital letters beginning each chapter, Thackeray produced nearly 200 images for his masterpiece (or, as he called his drawings, "candles for the performance"). On the cover of the twenty serialised "parts" of the novel, the book is called <u>Vanity Fair: Pen and Pencil Sketches of English Society</u>. Thackeray called himself a "twentieth-rate draughtsman," and many people, including myself, are unhappy with some of the large plates (his many renderings of Becky Sharp's face are especially harsh). However, if the full-page plates seem laboured, the small, apparently casual drawings that he dropped into stipulated points in his story are usually charming. The pictorial capitals with which he begins each chapter are superb; they are often thematic or symbolic or allegorical (as Trollope seems to be saying). Thackerayans have argued persuasively that these capitals are truly part of the text and ought to be incorporated even in modern editions that omit the larger drawings.

I send you one such capital from an early chapter (number 4) where Becky Sharp tries, cleverly though unsuccessfully, to ensnare fat Jos Sedley into marrying her. It doesn't "illustrate" a literal episode; and the sweetness of the little girl fishing for the fat fish is ironic.

Make sure the edition you read of <u>Vanity Fair</u> reproduces the original illustrations. With them, it's a different and better book, in my opinion.

Best
Stephen

Doesn't Trollope say anything about Millais, who is one of my favourite illustrators?

From: L.Dickerson@verizon.net
To: Nicholls@btinternet.com
April 25, 2007

Dear Stephen

He sure does mention Millais. About ten years later my gggf is cross-examining Trollope about illustrations to his own novels and complaining that the drawings coming out right then serially for <u>The Way We Live Now</u> are actually "defacing" the book:

39, Montagu Square

March 6, 1875

Dear MacDowell

After 1870, and after Millais was too busy to illustrate my novels (not that I blame him), I have often paid little attention to the illustrations in my books. As for those coming out at present in <u>The Way We Live Now</u>, I have positively thrown up my hands. The stiff, awkward figures, ugly faces, contorted limbs, and paw-like hands are beneath contempt. But what can I do? I wish to put my books into as many hands as possible, and if publishers insist on illustrations and these particular illustrators, there is next to nothing that I can do about it. The publishers of course pay for the illustrations.

Of the many novels I have published since <u>Framley Parsonage</u>, I think only one or two came out the old-fashioned way, i.e. without illustrations. I have never had an illustrator draw for more than one of my books — except for Millais.

I was most fortunate to have Millais illustrate four novels of mine during the sixties. As I have just said, the choice of illustrator is most often in the gift of the publisher or the magazine editor involved. When I heard that Millais was to illustrate <u>Framley Parsonage</u>, my first novel for the <u>Cornhill Magazine</u> and my first serial, I was thrilled. Millais is one of the great artists of our day. It was George Smith, the publisher of the <u>Cornhill</u>, that got him to illustrate <u>Framley</u> and <u>The Small House</u>.

Edward Chapman — at my urging — secured him for <u>Orley Farm</u>. By the time I came to edit (however abortively) my own magazine, I was able to draw on Millais's friendship and convince him to illustrate my own novel <u>Phineas Finn</u>. Of the four, my preference — and I would think anyone else's preference who cares about such things — is for the <u>Orley Farm</u> illustrations: the forty or so full-page "plates" Millais drew for that very long novel are I think the best for any novel in any language. I say that as a lover of art. As a writer I declare that he was absolutely conscientious, I could even say scrupulous, in being true to the passage he was illustrating. Don't ask me to pick a favourite among the forty — all those of Lady Mason and old Sir Peregrine Orme are excellent. Of course, as a passionate devotee of the hunt and someone who drags a hunting chapter or two into his novels wherever he can, I am partial to "Monkton Grange." But all the <u>Orley Farm</u> drawings are excellent.

As for Browne's illustrations to Dickens, I am rather lukewarm about them. On the other hand, you could say they suited Dickens admirably. Edward Chapman once hired Browne to illustrate a book of mine, <u>Can You Forgive Her?</u>, but Browne paid so little attention to the writing that I managed to get him replaced halfway through. The characters he drew all looked like they were Dickens characters that had managed to stray onto my pages.

Yours Sincerely
Anthony Trollope

Now for a dumb question. Who the hell is this Millais? I thought the name sounded like the Frenchman who painted a picture called The Man with a Hoe. Back in Junior High School they made us memorize a poem about the picture, part of which says "Whose was the hand that slanted back that brow?" I forget the name of the poet — am I on the right track here?

Yours
Larry

From: Nicholls@btinternet.com
To: L.Dickerson@verizon.net
26 April 2007

Dear Larry

John Everett Millais was an English painter and illustrator. "The Man
with the Hoe" was a painting by a Frenchman, Jean François Millet, and
the line you quote (very accurately) is from an American poet named
Edwin Markham. But I love the Trollope letter giving his opinion of
Browne, Millais, and his later 1870s illustrators. I'll "shoot" over to you
Millais's "Mockton Grange" illustration from Orley Farm.

Looking at this Millais drawing, you will quickly see how radically different it is from the Cruikshank and Browne illustrations to Dickens. Millais is the quintessential "Sixties" (the 1860s) artist. He was one of the original English "Pre-Raphaelites," and he strove for pictorial realism and accuracy, a realism that most people think was ideally suited to the kind of down-to-earth everyday realism that Trollope was famous for. (Not everyone liked Trollope's realism or that of the Pre-Raphaelites; one critic sneeringly called Trollope a "Pre-Raphaelite in prose.") Pre-Raphaelitism is notoriously difficult to define, beyond saying that it sought a close fidelity to nature and never (at least deliberately) wandered into caricature. So, even as Cruikshank and Phiz were well suited to Dickens, so Millais seems perfectly suited to Trollope.

Moreover, not only are the earlier and later drawings done in radically different styles, they were printed by radically different mechanisms. The Cruikshank and Browne drawings, often called "steel engravings," are in fact etchings. The artist draws with an etcher's needle (and in reverse) on a steel plate covered with a wax ground; acid is then applied to the wax ground to eat into the steel plate, leaving the lines in grooves; the wax is removed, ink is forced into the grooves, the excess ink wiped away (by hand); and the plate must be printed ("intaglio printing") separately from the letter press. The other kind of printing, associated mostly with the "Sixties," was wood engraving, and is exemplified in the Millais drawing. Wood engraving is, as I say, radically different from etching. The artist draws in pencil (again in reverse) on the end grain of a very hard wood, like boxwood; next a wood engraver (whose name gets equal billing on the finished product – often as here the Brothers Dalziel) cuts away with engraver's tools the parts of the drawing that are to appear white (it's called, a little strangely, "white line" engraving); the engraver leaves standing the lines that are to take ink and appear in black. This plate is printed exactly like letter press, that is to say, the ink is applied to the raised lines – like the letters on old typewriters. You will see immediately that this was a far easier way of printing drawings, because wood engraving did not require a separate process; a drawing could be "dropped in" anywhere amid the letter press. And indeed, where a book had both full-page steel plates and also small in-text drawings and pictorial capital letters (as in Thackeray), these smaller drawings <u>had</u> to be wood engraved.

As you would say, that's a hell of a lot longer answer than you bargained for, and even so it is drastically oversimplified.

Best
Stephen

From: L.Dickerson@verizon.net
To: Nicholls@btinternet.com
April 27, 2007

Dear Stephen

    Jesus, thanks for getting me to the right person. The Man with the Hoe business missed it by a mile. So thanks for cluing me in. I admit I had to read your description of etchings vs. wood engravings over two or three times, but I think I got it straight.

                                        Yours
                                        Larry

    Just straighten me out on one more thing. Is "serialization in parts" the same as "magazine serialization"?

From: Nicholls@btinternet.com
To: L.Dickerson@verizon.net
28 April 2007

Dear Larry

No. The great illustrated novels of this era were all serial novels –
appearing first in installments, either in issues of illustrated magazines
or in independent monthly "parts." Each monthly part (or "number")
had an illustrated cover, two full-page plates, about thirty pages of letter
press, and some advertisements; a part cost one shilling (twenty
shillings to the pound). Thus, big novels in parts, like Dickens's Pickwick
Papers (which got the whole business started) or David Copperfield or
Thackeray's Vanity Fair or Trollope's Orley Farm, were serialised
monthly over a long period – a little more than a year and a half. Once
serialisation was complete, the publisher would carry over the
illustrations into the first book editions, usually printed in two very large
volumes. These extra-long novels were the equivalent of five "volumes"
as measured against the otherwise standard Victorian three-volume or
"three-decker" novel. The Victorian reader saw these long novels
serialised in parts as a bargain compared to the usual three-decker
novel: they cost less, 20 shillings vs 31 shillings; were 2/5ths longer; and
provided forty plates (three-decker novels were almost never
illustrated). And your typical Victorian reader loved illustrations.

That's all, I promise.

Best
Stephen

From: L.Dickerson@verizon.net
To: Nicholls@btinternet.com
April 28, 2007

Dear Stephen

Do you know that in your enthusiasm you are lapsing into underlining for emphasis? Thanks for all the info on illustrating, printing, serializing, old style, Sixties style etc etc. I think I can say that with your help I get the picture. Ha!

However, as an old banker I can tell you that, from your account of 5 vs 3 volume novels, while the three decker is 2/5ths shorter than the five volume novel, the 5 volume novel is in fact 2/3rds longer than the 3 volume novel. Are you impressed? I hope so.

To come back down to earth, I hope this added interest of yours is also an added interest for the buyers of the letters.

Here's something for you: Gross, on finishing up Trollope, handed out a xerox of the last page of a long essay on Trollope written by your Henry James right after Trollope's death. James closes this essay with what Gross calls a very important observation about novels in general. James says that there are two kinds of taste in appreciating novels: "the taste for emotions of surprise and the taste for emotions of recognition." Of course Trollope "gratifies the taste for recognition" as opposed to the taste for surprise (as in Dickens, or, at the low end, in mysteries or thrillers or even in Wilkie Collins). We recognize ourselves in Trollope. Gross ended this class on Trollope quoting Virginia Woolf saying that "We believe in Trollope's characters the way we believe in our weekly bills," and that reading Trollope "is like watching something actually happen in the street below."

Yours
Larry

A small point — back to that Latin of a week or so back — so why doesn't Trollope just say "Art is to conceal art"?

From: Nicholls@btinternet.com
To: L.Dickerson@verizon.net
29 April 2007

Dear Larry

I had to read <u>your</u> account of the 2/5s vs 2/3s three times myself, and I stand impressed and corrected. It's kind of counter-intuitive, but then math often is.

You'll be pleased to know that Trollope letters are commanding very good prices and that ones like yours, with real content, have not been on the market for years.

The Henry James bit is lovely.

Here's a Trollope anecdote for you. John Major, when he was prime minister, went on a popular radio programme here called Desert Island Discs that asked famous people which book (other than the Bible and Shakespeare) they would take with them to a desert island, and John Major said Trollope's <u>The Small House at Allington</u> (whether with or without Millais's illustrations I don't know). Some critics professed to be shocked, while others said they knew what he meant. One columnist, I forget which, quoted the same Virginia Woolf as saying that <u>Pride and Prejudice</u> and <u>The Small House</u> were the "perfect novels" in the old-fashioned, traditional manner.

Best
Stephen

On the Latin: good question, why doesn't he just use the English? I think <u>Ars celare artem</u> is a famous old classical Latin quotation. (And, by the way, foreign words, like book titles, are usually underlined or italicised.) But, generally, you are absolutely correct. One should use foreign language phrases and words only when there is no accurate English equivalent.

⟶

From: L.Dickerson@verizon.net
To: Nicholls@btinternet.com
April 29, 2007

Stephen

That John Major story is a good one. I must look into that <u>Small House</u> book sometime soon. Problem is, as you put it to me months ago – in Latin – art is long and life is brief.

I still don't see why we don't have a good English phrase for <u>everything</u>. (The underlining there is for emphasis.) I was once going into a deli in the Bronx, and the guy I was with held the door for an attractive young woman and said, "Apres vous," and she shot him a dirty look as if to say, "Don't go using any filthy language on me, fella." Better to keep to English.

Tell me off the top of your head some foreign words we don't have good English for.

Larry

⟶

From: Nicholls@btinternet.com
To: L.Dickerson@verizon.net
30 April 2007

How about?
        coup d'état
        ad hoc
        ad hominem
        Weltanschauung

alta cocker (spelling?)
folie à deux

⟶

From: L.Dickerson@verizon.net
To: Nicholls@btinternet.com
April 30, 2007

Dear Foreign Language Adviser:

Coup d'etat I actually knew — a takeover of a government. I can't do accents.

And I have a vague sense of ad hoc — one time only.

Ad hominem — attacking the bastard himself instead of his arguments. Wouldn't "personal attack" do just as well?

I had to check out the others. Weltanschauung. I looked it up, and the word means "world view" in German, so why not just say "world view"? Actually I got the answer by looking in the big, unabridged dictionary: the German word can imply a whole "philosophy of life" and even "an interpretation of the universe," and so the meaning in German is wider than just "world view." Okay, so I give you that one, if only I could spell it by myself.

I find alta cocker is Yiddish — and it's a word you do hear around here occasionally — for an old fart who's always complaining. But nobody among my acquaintances knows for sure how to spell it. Alta cocker is close enough. I'm told the original means an "old shitter." Stephen, you surprise me, using language like that.

Finally, I certainly never heard of a folie a deux: It's "a condition in which symptoms of a mental disorder occur simultaneously in two people who share a close association." As far as I can tell, we don't have the word here and we don't even have the disease itself — not in America.

Yours
Larry

Chapter Eight

From: L.Dickerson@verizon.net
To: Nicholls@btinternet.com
May 2, 2007

Dear Stephen

Alright, I'm moving on to George Eliot and a novel – The Mill on the Floss – so autobiographical that it fits perfectly with Gross's idea about all novels being autobiographical but some of them being obviously more autobiographical than others. Mary Ann (later Marian) Evans was of course one of the smartest persons, man or woman, of her day. She spent all her life being especially devoted to one man – one at a time.

The first 35 years were a waste in this regard.

First, when she was a child, it was her older brother Isaac – a real shit, as we say over here, pardon my language.

Then it was her father in retirement and with him she had a long ruckus after she rejected Christianity.

And then a strange nut case called Dr. Brabant, who she was supposed to be helping as a kind of secretary – his wife has her kicked out of the house.

Then Mary Ann moved to London (by now she's Marian) and became overly "devoted" to a publisher named John Chapman for whom she was an assistant editor on a liberal magazine, The Westminster Review. So Chapman's wife and mistress have her kicked out of the house.

Next she falls in love with the philosopher Herbert Spencer, who was not the marrying kind.

Then, finally, she is attracted to the real thing – George Henry Lewes, another free thinker like Chapman and Spencer – and like herself. But Lewes was married to a woman named Agnes who bore him three children – and then this Agnes had three or four more children with a man named Thornton Hunt, a friend and colleague of Lewes's on a left wing magazine, <u>The Leader</u>. Lewes believed marriage only lasted while people were in love, and he acted very generously to his wife and to Hunt, and for the rest of his life Lewes supported not only his own three children but Hunt's four with Agnes. And Hunt kept having children by his own wife at the same time. Talk about the Victorians. I'm not making this up, I have my notes from Gross in front of me, and I've read about it in the biography by Gordon Haight, one of the books I bought at the Strand Bookstore. Divorce for Lewes was impossible, and after a year or so, Lewes and Marian decide to live together as husband and wife. And so they "elope" on a boat to the Continent and go to a place in Germany called Weimar.

When this news got back to their London circles all hell broke loose. Even the free thinkers were angry because they thought that having two of their own kind do this sort of thing would hurt the cause of liberalism in the country. Everyone thought Lewes would leave her after a while – he had a reputation for a "colorful" lifestyle and for telling dirty jokes in mixed company. Anyway, so all "literary" London was buzzing about the "blackguard Lewes and his whore." Lewes didn't give a damn about criticism of him, whereas she was very "thinskinned." Here she was going from being referred to as the "strong minded woman" who helped edit an important magazine to being called an infidel, concubine, adulterer, and "soiled woman." She and Lewes were "stink pots of humanity," living in a "cesspool." Even friends of hers backed away. Her tight-assed brother Isaac, head of the family, would not allow any of her family or relatives to communicate with her. Good hearted Mrs. Gaskell, a pretty open minded Unitarian, wrote a few years later to my gggf telling him that she – Mrs. Gaskell – had written to Marian saying "I wish you <u>were</u> Mrs. Lewes."

For years people would invite George Lewes to their homes, but never the fallen woman. But then, because of the novels she wrote, people slowly but surely started to want to go and see her at her house called "The Priory" near Regents Park, wherever that is. (I have letters with "The Priory" address printed on them.) And, as you say, in due course, eventually all sorts of people wanted to get in to meet her and be allowed to sit for a few minutes by the side of the "Great Teacher." (She got so famous that people started calling Lewes "Mr. George Eliot," and in our own times, "Best Actor in a Supporting Role.") An invitation to the Priory on Sunday afternoons became like getting a pass for a private audience with the pope, or as we say over here, it was the hottest ticket in town.

Now Stephen, listen to this description of George Eliot that I found in Gordon Haight's book. The description is by Henry James, who someone took along to The Priory to meet "the Wise Woman." James from what I can find out sounds like a piece of work. Anyway, in a letter to his father, here's how he describes visiting George Eliot:

> To begin with she is magnificently ugly – deliciously hideous. She has a low forehead, a dull grey eye, a vast pendulous nose, a huge mouth, full of uneven teeth, and a chin and jaw bone qui n'en finissent pas.... Now in this vast ugliness resides a most powerful beauty which, in a very few minutes steals forth and charms the mind so that you end up as I ended, in falling in love with her. Yes, behold me literally in love with this great horse-faced blue-stocking. A delightful expression, a voice soft and rich as that of a counseling angel – a mingled sagacity and sweetness, a broad hint of a great underlying world of reserve, knowledge, pride and power – a great feminine dignity and character in these massively plain features – a hundred conflicting shades of consciousness and simpleness – shyness and frankness – graciousness and remote indifference – these are some of the more definite elements of her personality. Her manner is extremely good though rather too intense and her speech, in the way of accent and syntax peculiarly agreeable. Altogether, she has a larger circumference than any woman I have ever seen.

"Larger circumference." What the hell kind of thing is that to say? She wasn't fat, that's about the one thing she wasn't in the bad looks department. Do you really think George Eliot was "colossally ugly" like they were saying? I email you a drawing of her (I'm getting pretty good at computers). The drawing is from 1865, so she was about 46. But now I find out – again in Gordon Haight – that the artist, Frederic Burton, him who drew the portrait, was a very good friend of hers. Also that he did many studies over a whole year so as to get one that "would satisfy the artist, the subject, and her friends." Of course he would go easy on her face, right? It says it's in chalk – how could a chalk drawing take a year?

Not that her looks matter, really. She could write, and more importantly, she could think. It dawns on me – and it's sad that this comes to me so late in the game, after so many months – it dawns on me now that a good novelist must not only be able to write, he, I mean he or she, must be able to think – he must have something to say.

Yours
Larry

I can guess the French – not finishing.
"Blue stocking" I had to look up.

From: Nicholls@btinternet.com
To: L.Dickerson@verizon.net
3 May 2007

Dear Larry

By now you know more about George Eliot than anyone I know. The
drawing came through fine. I see it is from the National Portrait Gallery.
Burton is a fairly well-respected second-tier artist, and his works fetch
good prices at auction, especially in recent years, as the market for
formerly neglected Victorian artists surges.

Best
Stephen

And the George Eliot letters themselves?

From: L.Dickerson@verizon.net
To: Nicholls@btinternet.com
May 6, 2007

Dear Stephen

Thanks. Unless of course you don't know anyone who knows
anything about her. In any case thanks for listening. My pals around
here couldn't care less about such things.

Right. The actual letters themselves. I'm sorry to say that most of
what I thought at first were George Eliot letters were from Lewes, not
from her. And his first two are about Darwin – Lewes was interested in
science of all kinds. But then my gggf gets him to write about <u>The Mill
on the Floss</u>, this very autobiographical novel. Lewes explains to my
gggf that his wife is "an intensely private person and extremely sensitive
to criticism about her fiction – even laudatory criticism. She absolutely
cringes at the merest hint of flattery." So she wouldn't go into the kinds

of questions my gggf was asking. Lewes himself can give only a very "partial" answer to my gggf's questions about <u>The Mill on the Floss</u> being about her herself and her brother. Lewes writes:

16, Blandford Square,
N.W.

3 Feb 1882

Dear MacDowell

    Of course everyone sees <u>The Mill on the Floss</u> *as "autobiographical." To which I say yes and no. Certainly there is in Maggie Tulliver a lot of Mrs. Lewes when she was a young girl growing up in Warwickshire. But of course it's a novel. For that matter, most "autobiographies" are novelistic.*
    You are not the only one to find the last part of the book less successful than the first parts. My wife herself is of that mind. The ending, with Maggie and her thick-headed brother united at last – but united only in death by drowning – has been seen by some critics, even by otherwise very appreciative critics of my wife's fiction, as a falling back on a deus ex machina resolution. But that's too facile. The book has prepared the reader for the possibility of Maggie's drowning. Perhaps it's true that in Maggie's case – to speak of her as if she were a real person – she seems to have been boxed in by fate <u>and</u> by her own character. She does go off with Stephen Guest but she refused to be intimate with him or to stay with him. Yet by a terrible irony, her fate is the worse back home for not having done so. We won't solve the conundrum here.

Yours truly
G H Lewes

    Do you think I should put in brackets an explanation of deus ex machina? Which of course I had to look up.

Larry

From: Nicholls@btinternet.com
To: L.Dickerson@verizon.net
8 May 2007

Larry

It's a very good letter, even if it's only from the "husband."

No, no brackets for deus ex machina.

Stephen

From: L.Dickerson@verizon.net
To: Nicholls@btinternet.com
May 15, 2007

Dear Stephen

    By now I've read <u>The Mill on the Floss</u> and also read plenty about it
in the biographies. Myself, I agree with those who say the early parts of
the novel showing the childhood of the heroine Maggie are "luminous"
(great word, right?). This first section is supposed to be as good as
anything in any Victorian novel along those lines. Even equal to
Dickens, who is a kind of specialist par excellence on children,
especially abused children. But the problem with the <u>last</u> part of the
book is that Maggie goes off briefly with Stephen Guest in a boat, sort
of like the way Marian Evans eloped on that boat to the Continent with
a married man. But as I get it, the problem is that Stephen Guest is no
G. H. Lewes. Lewes was the perfect soul mate for Marian Evans, but
Stephen Guest is not the perfect soul mate for Maggie. The cripple
hunchback Philip Wakem would have been the soul mate for her, but,
well, that wasn't in the cards. But even more important, Maggie Tulliver

is no Marian Evans, no George Eliot. Readers back then and even now expect Maggie to be like George Eliot and she can't because she isn't George Eliot or Mrs. Lewes or whatever we want to call her. Besides, if in the book Maggie behaved like George Eliot, no reputable publisher would have touched the book with a ten foot pole. Certainly not that fuddy duddy Scottish publisher of hers, John Blackwood. The way I see it, Maggie and Mary Ann Evans are similar, being girls much quicker mentally than their brothers. But we can't expect Maggie to do what the author did. Mary Ann – or Marian – Evans had it in her to go against public opinion and cause an uproar by going off and living with a married man. After that, as she herself wrote in a letter, she "never got invited to dinner," even by friends. That big asshole her brother Isaac Evans (Tom in the novel) only spoke to her 25 years later (and then only in writing through a lawyer) after Lewes had died and George Eliot went and married a banker, a man twenty years younger than her. By legally marrying she became "respectable" again. And this banker threw himself out of a window into the Canal at Venice on their honeymoon – a "temporary aberration." Talk about a soap opera.

How's all that for "context"? Pretty good for an old bank slogger, isn't it? Well, I can read and I can learn.

Yours
Larry

To: L.Dickerson@verizon.net
From: Nicholls@btinternet.com
16 May 2007

Larry

I am indeed impressed. Any good material from George Eliot herself? Please keep at those transcriptions.

Stephen

From: L.Dickerson@verizon.net
To: Nicholls@btinternet.com
May 17, 2007

I am keeping at them.

As I told you, Lewes answers most of my gggf's inquiries. In fact here's one about illustrations:

> The Priory
> 21. North Bank
> Regents Park

3 January 1865

Dear MacDowell

Both my wife and I were delighted with the choice of Frederic Leighton to do the illustrations in the Cornhill Magazine for her novel of fifteenth-century Florence. After all, Leighton knew Florence by heart, having lived and studied there. He worked most assiduously at the drawings, and, incidentally, he suffered self-described "agonies" at what the engravers did with his drawings. My wife made suggestions and criticisms and also lavished him with praise wherever she could honestly do so. She suggested everything from the tilt of a character's head to the shape of a woman's velvet birretta, telling him at one point, if I remember correctly, that he might consult the engravings of Ghirlandajo's frescoes as to women's hats. Leighton did his best. But after a while it became clear to her that the task of illustrating a novel such as Romola was in itself impossible (unless the illustrations be limited to architectural drawings – which of course would not have suited the publisher, George Smith). That is to say, she came to realise that the effort to bring about what she called "a perfect correspondence" between her intentions and the illustrations was hopeless – for Leighton or anyone else. She concluded, and I recall her very words – to me, not to Leighton –

that illustrations can form at best only "a kind of overture" to the text.
    She saw to it that the plates were not carried over to the book edition.

Ever yours
G H Lewes

But very late in the game — 1873 — George Eliot herself writes:

The Priory
21. North Bank
Regents Park

27 April 1873

Dear Mr MacDowell,

    My husband tells me you are a most attentive student of the contemporary novel and begs me to answer your kind letter in some detail. He tells me you have corresponded on these issues with Thackeray, Dickens, Anthony Trollope, and others. Of Dickens, about whom you especially ask, I am of somewhat mixed mind. He was of course a genius. He is a master of language, and he comes up with similes and metaphors that no one else on earth could devise. And then he has a way of staying with that metaphor in subsequent pages — a person's mouth becomes a postal box, and then the person himself turns into a post office, etc. He is as droll as anyone who has ever written in English. I love his "minor" characters — Sam Weller, Mrs Gamp, Mr Toots, Mr Micawber, Mr Dick, Mr Pumblechook, Trabb's boy — these are beyond the reach of anyone alive or dead, in my view. Charles Dickens was the most imaginative — always excepting Shakespeare — writer in our tongue. My husband, who knew him well, published an article saying that Dickens told him that he <u>heard</u> every word his characters said. George gave it as his opinion that in some peculiar way Mr Dickens was not speaking figuratively. He thought Dickens an exceptional man in many ways and even a peculiar man, as geniuses usually are. My husband may have tested the patience of Dickens's disciples (and they are <u>disciples</u>) when in this article he said that Dickens while creating underwent such identification with his characters, especially his peculiar characters and especially when he has them speak in dialogue, that he was in some way "hallucinating." As you probably know, Mr Forster, in his Life of Dickens, took great umbrage and replied in a scathing way. My husband and Forster are no longer on speaking terms. What can one say? When one writes, he exposes himself to the public and to public outrage or adulation. George has such broad knowledge and such careful thinking that I fear many people cannot really grasp just what it is that he is saying.

But it is only fair for me to say – and these lines are of course private and intended for your eyes only – that Dickens lacks a concern for what I have called the suppressed transitions in human behaviour. He really does think that people for the most part are either terribly good or terribly bad. This means his characters are often two-dimensional. Now, his two dimensions are worth more than other people's multiple dimensions. To call them cartoon characters is to miss the point. He wants many of them to be caricatures – in the best sense of that word, even as to have produced the greatest line drawings in the world is better than to have produced many mediocre oil paintings with numerous shades of colouring. Still, this means that Dickens misses the intermediatenesses, the grey areas in personalities. But perhaps he wanted to miss them. Perhaps he meant to create glorious fables or myths and not "realistic" stories. I say this as one who has tried, and often failed, at the latter. Dickens's young heroines are his weakest characters. He simply can not or will not portray a young woman who is flesh and blood. A friend of mine once remarked rather coarsely that at the end of <u>David Copperfield</u>, the hero is driven into the arms of Agnes Wakefield – "if she has arms." And the very close of the novel, with her inspiring him to look up to heaven, doesn't sit well with me, though I think the book on the whole one of his best. I don't care for the way Dickens brings Christianity into his texts every now and then. These inclusions seem slightly askew, off kilter. They are, I think, rather <u>pro forma</u>, as if the author felt obliged to say these things *while not himself being overly convinced of them. Of course I don't know this, but that is what I sense in reading him.*

Thackeray: another genius, but sometimes a rather flippant one and nowhere near as <u>even</u> a writer as his great rival Dickens. On the other hand, I, like many others, see <u>Vanity Fair</u> as a high peak. My husband feels the same way. (George, ever since Thackeray's <u>Snob Papers</u> appeared in the eighteen forties, thinks that Thackeray <u>as writer</u>, not necessarily as novelist, is at the very top of the tree.) Some people find <u>Vanity Fair</u> deeply cynical; others (in a view I feel is utterly wrong-headed) think it is exceedingly sentimental. The narrator is in my opinion occasionally a little too arch, and in this I am told that he is very like the man Thackeray himself, who was capable of considerable pessimism about humanity. (I am also assured by my husband and by Anthony Trollope, both of whom knew him well, that Thackeray's negative side was all on the surface and that he was, underneath, the kindest and gentlest of men.) As for Thackeray's less than sanguine view of human nature, he argues his case brilliantly in <u>Vanity Fair</u>. I myself would hope he were wrong, but on so unwieldy an issue no one can know anything — anything compelling — beyond his own convictions. <u>Vanity Fair</u> is a big book in all senses. In the argument about assigning "first place" among English novelists, I have heard it said that "educated" and "intellectual" people tend to favour Thackeray over Dickens, but I myself hesitate to enter into this kind of weighting. The question cannot be answered. The writers are too different in what they do and how they do it to warrant any ranking.

Briefly, as this letter is becoming long enough to weary both of us, I add but a quick word as to our friend Anthony Trollope. I am myself acquainted with many of his novels (no one could keep up with <u>all</u> he writes). In those I have read I find careful delineation of character, realistic speech, and what might be called ordinary, every-day plots. But what most interests me is the bracing air that pervades his books; they are filled with belief in goodness without the slightest tinge of maudlin. As I once told him, his novels remind me of open, *pleasant public gardens, where people go for recreation but without knowing it get health as well, such is the excellent moral atmosphere that his fiction exudes. This may sound rather preachy, but it is what I feel – and I can't help but think that Mr Trollope himself feels this way too.*

Yours faithfully
M. E. Lewes

My gggf sent her a special note of thanks, but he never heard from her again. By this time people were saying that she wrote "novels for philosophers." Not very high praise if you ask me. Some people thought she was up there with Shakespeare and with the Prophet Elijah. So even if at first I was disappointed to find G. H. Lewes answering my gggf's George Eliot letters, I think this one makes up for it. What do you think?

Yours
Larry

〈 ⌒〉

From: Nicholls@btinternet.com
To: L.Dickerson@verizon.net
18 May 2007

Larry

It's a spectacular letter. It's a shame all nineteen "Eliot" letters are not from her – and like this one.

Stephen

⌒〉

From: L.Dickerson@verizon.net
To: Nicholls@btinternet.com
May 18, 2007

Dear Stephen,

　　Well, we work with what we got, right? No use crying over spilt milk, as they say. Though it's not really spilt milk, come to think of it, because that would have been if my gggf had had more letters from her and they got lost or destroyed.

Yours
Larry

Chapter Nine

From: L.Dickerson@verizon.net
To: Nicholls@btinternet.com
May 20, 2007

Dear Stephen

I hope you haven't forgotten that I have Darwin letters. My New School instructor says he knows next to nothing about evolution itself beyond what the ordinary slob knows. Also, I think he was getting just a little tired of me pestering him after class. So I just have you to pester.

My real trouble concerns Darwinism — just <u>exactly</u> what it was, and also how long it took to catch on. Like everybody else of course I know about one animal evolving into another and that men look like apes and that birds and fish are related to us, two wings, two fins, two arms, etc. But not many people, including yours truly, know anything substantial about how evolution works. Any help?

Yours
Larry

From: Nicholls@btinternet.com
To: L.Dickerson@verizon.net
21 May 2007

Larry

Darwin is beyond my ken except in a most elementary fashion. Sorry. Did I know the subject, I'd play the pedant for you.

Stephen

From: L.Dickerson@verizon.net
To: Nicholls@btinternet.com
May 22, 2007

Dear Stephen

Fair enough. Could you recommend someone in England who might be able to help me on this Darwin stuff? Darwin was an Englishman, and it seems to me an Englishman would know better how to explain evolution than some American professor sitting over here and claiming to be an expert.

Yours
Larry

From: Nicholls@btinternet.com
To: L.Dickerson@verizon.net
22 May 2007

Dear Larry

This is the first time you've said something foolish in all our long
epistolary conversation. There are plenty of capable American scholars.
Please don't become such an anglophile as to repudiate American
writers simply on the accident of place of birth. The leading scholars in
bringing Victorian novelists back into favour have been, for the most
part, Americans – you yourself mentioned Edgar Johnson for Dickens;
for Thackeray it's Gordon Ray; for George Eliot it's Gordon Haight –
and so on. Trollope too, though I can't think of the name at the
moment. And I'm sure it's just as true in the history of science.

Best
Stephen

From: L.Dickerson@verizon.net
To: Nicholls@btinternet.com
May 23, 2007

Stephen

   Are they all named Gordon? Sounds like a last name over here.
Though, come to think of it, I have a nephew named Gordon. So all
right, I take your point. Still, can you name someone who would shoot
the breeze with me via email on the occasional Darwin question?

                                        Larry

From: Nicholls@btinternet.com
To: L.Dickerson@verizon.net
24 May 2007

Dear Larry,

I don't know about shooting the breeze, as you put it, but I was at university with a very friendly and knowledgeable chap who became what is called a "don" or "fellow" at Lincoln College Oxford. He's in English literature but is interested in Darwin, and I imagine he knows the subject quite well. Promise you won't overdo it. He's terribly busy, and it wouldn't do to draw too frequently on his kindness. Try for answers yourself and save him for a court of final appeal. His name is Leonard Hill (don't call him "Leo" or "Len" – it's Leonard).

His email is: L.Hill@lincoln.ox.ac.uk.

You'll find him a very generous correspondent. Use my name of course, but as I have said, you shouldn't attempt to be in regular contact with him in the way that you are with me.

Best
Stephen

From: L.Dickerson@verizon.net
To: Nicholls@btinternet.com
May 25, 2007

Stephen

   Thanks. I got the picture. No problem. I won't hassle him with too many questions. He'll be my last resort. I'll hold off writing to him until I get a regular doozy of a puzzler.

                                                    Larry

From: L.Dickerson@verizon.net
To: L.Hill@lincoln.ox.ac.uk
May 25, 2007

Dear Don Leonard Hill,

Stephen Nicholls tells me you are an old buddy of his and wouldn't mind if I put a few questions to you. I am the self-appointed editor and "annotator" of about 220 letters to and from my great-great-grandfather from well known Victorian writers: Dickens, Thackeray, Charlotte Bronte (really from Mrs. Gaskell about Charlotte Bronte), Wilkie Collins, Trollope, Hardy, and – from what I have picked up – a regular smart aleck named Samuel Butler. I inherited these via my mother's family, and in my retirement after being for many years a bank worker, I'm working on these letters for eventual selling through Stephen at Christie's. He'll vouch for me. I am cooking up my own transcriptions and annotations to the letters for a little book of my own for private consumption. Stephen said you knew the Victorian period inside out and wouldn't mind if I put a question or two to you to see if you might help me out in regard to Darwin. Because among all these letters from novelists there are some letters from Darwin. Stephen says Darwin is a side line with you, and he admits he can't help me on Darwin.

Here's my question. It's a big one but any help would be appreciated, greatly. Darwin – and my great-great-grandfather became a great fan of Darwin – published On the Origin of Species in 1859 (some people forget the "On" in the first edition).* Okay. How long did it take for his idea to really get around? Did it get quickly into the minds for example of those people I call "my" novelists as per named above? What did Dickens, Thackeray, and the rest of them think of evolution? And, next, and maybe this should be first, can you also tell me in simple words just what the hell evolution really is? I mean I know what evolution is in a general way. But when I looked into Darwin's actual books, they were too rough going for me. And the modern books on it are pretty steep too. Just please give me the kind of answer you might give to someone who asked you out of the blue at a party to tell them just what Darwin evolution is.

I don't want to be intruding on your time. Stephen tells me college professors are just as busy as other people even though I know that they get all sorts of vacations – like the entire summer off and January between semesters and also "sabbatical" leave for a year or so, with pay. Some of my bank customers were college professors and I sort of got to know them. Always going off to Europe or somewhere on summer vacations. Nice fellows, though, and one girl professor, too. Woman, I mean. At the bank I got two weeks vacation a year – three weeks after many years. But that is neither here nor there, of course. I'd be most appreciative of any light you can throw on Darwin for me.

Sincerely yours
Larry Dickerson

* Just showing off.

⟨⟩

From: L.Hill@lincoln.ox.ac.uk
To: L.Dickerson@verizon.net
28 May 2007

Dear Mr Dickerson,

Darwin did make something of a splash right from the beginning, but this was only with intellectuals and scientists, especially naturalists and geologists. He aroused the enmity of many clerics – though not all of them. It took a good deal longer for the issues he raised to get around to your average middle class men and women, people who read but were not scientists or intellectuals. The common view sometimes heard today that the <u>Origin</u> on its arrival in 1859 caused in the blink of an eye a revolution in human thought and turned religious thinking and even scientific thinking upside down is utterly false. Those who hold this innocent but erroneous conviction probably do so hoping that this were the case. It makes for a more exciting story – or "narrative," as we say – than the slow, book by book, year by year, decade by decade time that it actually took. But in about thirty years or so (these remarks are just informal estimates, so please don't quote me because it is not my field), Darwin and his theories were getting widely read and talked about.

As regards your novelists: I don't know that Thackeray or Dickens ever mentioned the subject. Mrs Gaskell knew Darwin's wife's family – the Wedgwoods – the Wedgwood China people. She was a Unitarian, and Unitarians can accommodate almost any belief or angle. She was friends with some Oxford liberals who sided with Darwin. There's a whiff of naturalist science in her great novel <u>Wives and Daughters</u>. Collins doesn't seem to have said anything about evolution (he was a freethinker in other regards, marriage, for instance). Trollope wrote to a would-be contributor to his magazine that he, Trollope, was lamentably ignorant of Darwinism and didn't want to publish a paper on the subject because he wouldn't know if the paper were sound or not. George Eliot, who was of a mind with her husband, G. H. Lewes, on most things, sympathised with Darwin's views. Hardy was a devoted follower of Darwin. Samuel Butler's case is difficult to tie down. After being an ardent champion of Darwin as a young man, he gradually, while remaining an evolutionist, disagreed more and more with Darwin. Butler wanted to see purpose – a teleology – in evolution. He also propounded the notion of an "unconscious memory" (derived from a universal "life force") that was inherited over millions of generations, bringing with it an instinctive wisdom, including a vague belief in something "supernatural," a belief which, the moment you put it to rational test or try to "demonstrate" it, withers away; indeed, he thought that in some mysterious way <u>everything</u> in the universe has an "unconscious memory." You will find Butler contradictory: at one moment saying things like "An honest God is the noblest work of man" and that "to love God is to have good health, good sense, and a fair balance of cash on hand," and arguing that organised Christianity was a "vast imposture" supporting a "gaggle of superstitions." Yet on the other hand you find him saying that the main ideas underlying orthodox faith are sound – as long as you don't try to tamper with them by "proving" things like the existence of God or the resurrection and ascension of Christ. Butler is ever the ironist, and you never know where you are with him.

As for your forthright question, just what the hell Darwinian evolution is, the starting point is to know that Darwinism has various components, and I'll dash off and underline as many as I can bring to mind:

Common descent of all living things from some first, single, living cell – the Family of Man, as it's called, is an actuality, and goes back through animal, plant, and cell life, and we are related not just to chimps and gorillas, but to ants and daisies and microbes.

Evolution happened gradually over huge periods of time, and the world was not some 6000 years old. (A Protestant Irish bishop named Ussher in the 1600s had calculated from the Bible that the creation of Adam happened in October, 4004 B.C. Pure nonsense, but a reckoning widely credited for more than two centuries and probably still believed by a few rabid biblical literalists.)

There are countless species because they have been forever multiplying, branching out, evolving.

Moreover, countless species have been going extinct for millions of years.

Finally, the manner in which new species come about is natural selection; namely, nature "selects" (a metaphor, of course) which of the mutations or changes in individuals are better "adapted" for survival in their environment; and these mutated, better-equipped individuals pass on their genes to their offspring. Giraffes survived because, with their long necks, they could get more food by feeding off the leaves at the tops of trees. In Darwin's thinking, the giraffes didn't get their long necks by stretching up for leaves; they got them by accidents of birth – some giraffes were born with longer necks – and nature "selected" these longer-necked giraffes to survive and pass on their long necks to their offspring. (Ernst Mayr, One Long Argument is very good on this.)

Now, implied in all this there were – there are – some dangerous ideas: that there was no designer or God (nature did the "designing" by selecting); that man really is not terribly different from other animals;

that the world and human beings have no built-in "purpose"; that, instead, there's a deuce of a lot of chance – <u>luck</u> – involved in every-thing. This view alarmed and "disenchanted" many people, especially Christians and other religious persons who wanted "meaning" built into their lives. The traditional Western perspective, embracing divine origin, purpose, immortality, etc, may be more "inspiring" and "helpful" and "hopeful," but it lacks reality, not of course in the sense that people don't really believe it and benefit from it, but in the sense that basically, at bottom, it's wrong; it doesn't conform to reality.

That's a longer answer than you bargained for, and I must run to a meeting.

I hope this is of some assistance, and good luck with your project.

Do give my best to Stephen Nicholls when next you write him.

Cordially
Leonard Hill

I won't comment on the busyness of university professors.

〈 ⁀ 〉

From: L.Dickerson@verizon.net
To: L.Hill@lincoln.ox.ac.uk
May 29, 2007

Dear Don Leonard Hill,

Thanks a million. That's a terrific help. I appreciate your really long answer. Now I'll know what I am talking about in reference to evolution. With that much in my head – and I have a good memory – I could hold my own with anyone who wanted to talk evolution with me, which they don't.

I nearly asked another question but have restrained myself.

Only joking about professors not being busy.

Yours sincerely
Larry Dickerson

From: L.Hill@lincoln.ox.ac.uk
To: Nicholls@btinternet.com
29 May 2007

Dear Stephen

   Your American sounds like quite the character. I gave him an inordinately lengthy answer – all vague commonplaces on the subject. But I shan't like to continue at that length. Do gently remind him not to keep feeding me questions. Just the occasional perplexity.

Always
Leonard

   He addressed me as "Don Leonard Hill."

From: Nicholls@btinternet.com
To: L.Hill@lincoln.ox.ac.uk
29 May 2007

Dear Leonard

Thanks so much. I'll call him off. You're lucky he didn't address you as "Dear Don Fellow Leonard Hill."

Yours always
Stephen

I trust all is well with you among the dreamy spires of Oxford.

From: Nicholls@btinternet.com
To: L.Dickerson@verizon.net
29 May 2007

Dear Larry

I understand Leonard Hill has been of help to you. Good, but please do not take offense when I reiterate what I said about not troubling him too much. You can look up many things on your own.

Best
Stephen

Please don't address him as "Don Leonard Hill."

⌣⃔

From: L.Dickerson@verizon.net
To: Nicholls@btinternet.com
May 30, 2007

Dear Stephen

Thanks, but don't worry. I won't pester him with questions and won't write again till something completely stumps me (and you).

But he really helped me on Darwin. His email was practically an article on the subject. Smart fellow. An unintentional pun. Fellow of his College and a smart fellow.

I'm sending you here – early – transcriptions of my two Darwin letters. I get so damn annoyed at seeing things in the papers about religious people wanting to put "Intelligent Design" up against Darwin in high school science textbooks. It makes me ashamed to be so much of an American. In any case, here are my two Darwin letters (one very short, as I've told you). I've looked into the Darwin letters at the library. Technically it's his "Correspondence" including all the letters to him – just like with my stuff. My god, with Darwin it's worse than with

Dickens. Big thick black volumes coming out for years now and they are at Volume 16 and only in the year 1868. That means they got 14 years to go, and he wrote more and more letters each year as he got more famous. Well, I got two Darwin letters, and they are after 1868, so maybe I should eventually send them to the editors. Talk about a drop in the bucket. But they are nice letters. And you'll notice that Darwin in his letters gives a month and day (American style, too) but never a year. We get the year – 1871 – from my gggf as he starts off the exchange by sending Darwin what we would today call a fan letter, which I won't trouble you with. But here's Darwin's reply:

> *Down. Bromley.*
> *Kent. S.E.*
> *April 5th*

Dear Sir

Thank you. It was thoughtful of you to write to me with such kind thoughts about my work. I have not much time for correspondence, given all my obligations to colleagues who write to me on matters of geology, botany, and my species theory. I will merely remark that with a parent's natural pride, I am pleased with the sentence and sentiments voiced in "There is grandeur in this view of life. . . ."

Yes, I have to proceed gingerly around conventional thinking, ancient traditions and beliefs that help so many people, while at the same time I try to introduce people to a new view of nature and of their place in that nature. I, and others who hold views like mine, must walk warily, not offending people, people to whom the old ways give support, purpose, and courage.

> *Believe me, my dear Sir*
> *Yours very sincerely*
> *C. Darwin*

Now, here's my gggf's next letter. It's more to the point than the reply from the great man himself:

Paternoster Row
London. E.C.

8 April 1871

Dear Mr Darwin

Thank you for your gracious letter.

I won't trespass on your time further except to remark that, granted, as you say, that many people are helped by the old ways (your not calling them religion is an example of your tact, something I often lack); granted that religion can give people hope and even sustenance; granted all this, is not the question a still more basic one: do religious beliefs conform to the facts of the natural world? If they don't, are we to suffer superstition and ignorance because it is good for people? Isn't <u>truth</u> good for people? Excuse the heat of my words. But I believe you who have done more than anyone, anywhere, to foster the scepticism I so wholeheartedly embrace. Now, with Natural Selection (I feel I must capitalise it as others capitalise Christianity), we non-believers in the supernatural have something positive, something rational and scientific, and with it a "certain grandeur" into the bargain, and — I'm repeating myself — all the grander for being true. And you'll excuse my saying so, it is by now much more than a "species theory." As far as I can tell, it's fact, laid out in paragraph after paragraph, chapter after chapter, in your magical writing.

Yours truly
Jeremy MacDowell

To this Darwin comes back with a short but sweet letter, the shortest letter in the whole collection:

Down. Bromley.
Kent. S.E
April 11th

Dear Mr MacDowell

Thank you. Thank you. As I have said, my writings form, I hope,
one long argument.

Yours sincerely
C. Darwin

On this letter my gggf penciled "CD is too gentle, too tactful, to
come right out and say I've hit the bull's eye, perhaps for fear I would
broadcast any frank statement of his own non-belief. But I take the two
thank yous as implying as much. Darwin is a great implier, as when he
says near the end of the <u>Origin</u> that doubtless this theory will throw
light on the origin of man and his history. I'll say it will."
Are you impressed? Are you bowled over?

Yours
Larry

⌐‿⌐

From: Nicholls@btinternet.com
To: L.Dickerson@verizon.net
2 June 2007

Larry

The Darwin exchanges are perfectly wonderful.

Stephen

⌐‿⌐

From: L.Dickerson@verizon.net
To: Nicholls@btinternet.com
June 15, 2007

Dear Stephen

    Following up on this Darwin business, can you tell me what "philosophical realism" is? I've been looking into a book your friend Hill recommended to me. And yes, I know I could "look it up," and in fact I did look it up but I am still in the dark.

                                               Larry

From: Nicholls@btinternet.com
To. L.DIckerson@verizon.net
16 June 2007

Dear Larry,

I don't know. Or if I did know, I forget. I was going to say you could look it up, but you have forestalled me there.

Stephen

From: L.Dickerson@verizon.net
To: Nicholls@btinternet.com
June 17, 2007

Stephen

    I know I "forestalled" you.
    By the way, did you know that over here "You could look it up" is a

famous saying in baseball and supposed to be funny? It's from a real character named Casey Stengel, a baseball team manager. Baseball is filled with statistics, more statistics than all the other sports put together, and people are forever being told they could look something up in the Record Book.

Larry

From: Nicholls@btinternet.com
To: L.Dickerson@verizon.net
18 June 2007

Dear Larry

I didn't know that. "You could look it up" seems to be a perfectly straightforward sentence. Why is there anything special about Mr Stengel's saying it?

How are the other transcriptions coming along?

Stephen

From: L.Dickerson@verizon.net
To: Nicholls@btinternet.com
June 19, 2007

Dear Stephen

There you go. I never heard anyone ever call Casey Stengel "Mr. Stengel." I guess what he said is considered funny because of the way he said it and under the circumstances. I think it was when reporters asked him after he had just had a losing season how he thought he would do next season and he told them they could look it up.

Larry

As I've told you, I'm working on the transcriptions as fast as humanly possible.

⌒

From: Nicholls@btinternet.com
To: L.Dickerson@verizon.net
21 June 2007

I'll never again call him Mr Stengel.

⌒

From: L.Dickerson@verizon.net
To: Nicholls@btinternet.com
June 22, 2007

Stephen

Hold the phone. I just looked up "You could look it up" on Google. A writer named James Thurber published a baseball story in 1941 called "You Could Look It Up" – about a midget playing baseball. But Stengel did say you could look it up, and I doubt he ever heard of Thurber. I never heard of him.

Larry

⌒

From: Nicholls@btinternet.com
To: L.Dickerson@verizon.net
23 June 2007

Dear Larry

I have you there. James Thurber was a fine writer and humourist who worked for The New Yorker and also drew many funny cartoons (often of animals) for the magazine. Christie's has handled some of his drawings at auction. A famous one has a woman sternly asking a hippopotamus that has just swallowed something, "Now what have you done with Dr. Millmoss?" Another shows a huge seal over the headboard of a couple in bed, and the man is saying to his wife, "Okay, have it your way. You heard a seal bark."

Best
Stephen

From: L.Dickerson@verizon.net
To: Nicholls@btinternet.com
June 24, 2007

Dear Stephen

Even though I live in New York, I only see The New Yorker in doctors' waiting rooms. And it looks too high brow for me, but I do go for their cartoons.

By the way, do you get a lot of crap you don't want in your email? Like everybody else over here I am sick of what we call spam in the U.S. Named after the cheap canned meat that servicemen got even when they didn't want it. Every day I get at least five messages from something calling itself Lifedreams promising to get me hooked up with the woman – or man – of my dreams.

Yours
Larry

⌒

From: Nicholls@btinternet.com
To: L.Dickerson@verizon.net
25 June 2007

Dear Larry

Of course we here in England have unwanted letters in our email called spam, but I think you'll find the word derives not from the Spam pressed meat – we have that too – but from British Television's "Monty Python's Flying Circus," where it was a kind of nonsense word, repeated endlessly.

Best
Stephen

⌒

From: L.Dickerson@verizon.net
To: Nicholls@btinternet.com
June 26, 2007

Dear Stephen

You're losing your advantage over me, my fine feathered friend. I just Googled spam. I find that the spam in Monty Python (the show came over here on public television) when it is first mentioned is the Spam you have with eggs and toast in the morning.

Larry

From: Nicholls@btinternet.com
To: L.Dickerson@verizon.net
28 June 2007

Larry

Thanks on the spam/Spam. I'll know better than ever to question your opinion, especially on things with American overtones.

Stephen

From: L.Dickerson@verizon.net
To: Nicholls@btinternet.com
June 29, 2007

Stephen

Jesus, I'm right once in a blue moon. Don't stop questioning me. But I'm still obsessing over that "realism" stuff.

Larry

From: L.Dickerson@verizon.net
To: L.Hill@lincoln.ox.ac.uk
June 29, 2007

Dear Leonard Hill,

Sorry to bother you again, but can you tell me what "philosophical realism" is? That man Mayr I've been looking into at your suggestion keeps saying Darwinism really put the kibosh to "philosophical realism" or "essentialism." I can't figure it out. Because everywhere I look I read that George Eliot and Trollope (and Thackeray, too) were great "realists." Where am I? I looked it up but — for me at least — the explanations don't work. I promise this is my last time bothering you, but Nicholls doesn't know the answer and just tells me to look it up, and as I say, I can't make head or tail of what I look up. Just a cocktail talk description would do me fine.

Thanks a million.

Sincerely yours
Larry Dickerson

From: L.Hill@lincoln.ox.ac.uk
To: L.Dickerson@verizon.net
3 July 2007

Dear Mr Dickerson,

Philosophical realism or essentialism has nothing to do with literary realism such as you are dealing with in the novels of George Eliot and Trollope. Literary realism presents the reader with characters who are very like the characters we "really" meet in everyday life — ordinary people, not fairy-tale heroes or supermen or monsters or devils; moreover, the stories in which these characters move (the plots) are of an ordinary "realistic" sort — not especially unusual or filled with impossible coincidences. Philosophical realism, on the other hand, is a doctrine that gives "real" existence to abstract ideas or "universals" — beauty, truth, triangles, and the so-called "essence" of anything, e.g., that which makes wine wine, or bread bread, or man man: "breadness" or "wineness" or "humanness." The medieval philosopher who best challenged this ancient nonsense was William of Occam, who said that notions like beauty, truth, etc were just names we gave to these abstractions or universals — hence the word "nominalism." You yourself are almost certainly a nominalist.

You are coming at this, I see, from the Darwinian point of view. You will see right away that Darwin, who dealt so much in particulars, would have nothing to do with immutable "essences" – closely allied, mutatis mutandis, to "immutable species" – which he saw as not immutable at all but as constantly evolving.

Now a word of advice. Forget it. Steer clear of this stuff. What I just said is a quick and sloppy version of arguments that have gone on forever. To my mind (and this is probably unfair to some modern philosophical realists), the discussion is about matters no more "real" than were the contests between the ancient Greek gods. In your project, don't get bogged down in the philosophical positions that Darwinism contradicted. Just know that you are a nominalist as opposed to a philosophical realist. Stay with your novelists. Keep your feet on the ground. "Earth's the right place."

Cordially
L. Hill

From: L.Dickerson@verizon.net
To: L.Hill@lincoln.ox.ac.uk
July 5, 2007

Dear Leonard Hill,

A thousand thanks. I'll follow your advice and forget it. And I won't be troubling you again. I hope not anyway.

Yours
Larry Dickerson
Nominalist

I had to check out "mutatis mutandis." Nice phrase.

From: L.Dickerson@verizon.net
To: Nicholls@btinternet.com
July 5, 2007

Stephen

    Where is "Earth's the right place" from? Poetry? Sounds familiar –
maybe from high school English class a hundred years ago.

                                    Larry

From: Nicholls@btinternet.com
To: L.Dickerson@verizon.net
6 July 2007

It's Robert Frost. "Birches."

Chapter Ten

From: L.Dickerson@verizon.net
To: Nicholls@btinternet.com
July 11, 2007

Dear Stephen

　　Maybe I've been spoiled by reading the good stuff. Just finished Wilkie Collins's <u>The Woman in White</u>. If he is the top of the second layer, I'd hate to have to read something from the bottom of that second layer, much less anything at all from the third or fourth layers. And speaking of layers and numbers, Gross says the authority on such matters – a man named Sutherland – estimates that there were about 60,000 novels published during the reign of Queen Victoria. That's a scary number, even if she did reign for a long time. So, we "students" of Dickens, Thackeray, the Brontes, George Eliot et al, even if we read all their novels – which nobody does – but even if we did, it would come to only about 130 novels. And if it weren't for Trollope's 47, it would be under a hundred. So today's so-called experts have probably read <u>at best</u> 100 or so of the 60,000 Victorian novels. I can do the math – from my bank days – and it's .2%! And .2% is a lot less than it sounds. If you read all the big names, for every book you read – say, for every <u>Oliver Twist</u> – there would be roughly 460 others you haven't read. I'm using a calculator of course.

　　Some advanced thinkers think the 100 good things have survived because of "class values" and the influence of teachers pushing the "canonical" books, etc. I say these good books have survived because they are good.

　　But back to Wilkie Collins. I had high expectations for <u>The Woman</u>

in White as "the greatest sensation novel ever written." It certainly had all sorts of sensational things in the plot: murders, forgeries, false commitments to lunatic asylums, faked wills, faked deaths, spies, secret Italian societies, mysterious illegitimate births, all sorts of surprises. As my old man would say, "one damn thing after another." Oh yes, and then a happy ending, the villain assassinated in Paris, the poor girl inheriting tons of money and marrying the hero and living happily ever after.

Here's my gggf going to town in his reading diary on The Woman in White:

> Disappointing. Perhaps the most ingenious plot ever conceived. But overwritten, too long, descriptions boring, the dialogue fair at best. Character of Fosco best thing in the book. Unless it be the old hypochondriac Frederick Fairlie. So Collins, for all his storytelling inventiveness, is not a good writer. Many of the sentences are wooden, with the predictable two adjectives for each noun. To put any page of Dickens or Thackeray up against him is Hyperion to a Satyr. Trollope, too, is a better writer, though in a very different fashion. Trollope writes so smoothly and so quietly that sometimes you are not even aware that some of his prose is "writing" – it's just reality coming straight at you. Of course some people think it too real, too much like actual life, and therefore boring. And George Eliot can be a poet in prose – although I don't like left-handed compliments to writers of prose. Give me Dickens, Thackeray, or Eliot any day against the "divine" Tennyson, the obscure Browning, or any other of today's poets. I remember Dickens having old Tony Weller tell his son "Poetry ain't natural."

> Collins himself, on the other hand, is the most pleasant of men, the jolliest of companions, a brave little fellow with all sorts of physical ailments who thumbs his nose at convention – like refusing ever to wear formal dress; more unconventional still, rumour says he lives with a working class woman and won't marry her because he thinks marriage demeans women.

That's the longest entry in my gggf's reading log. It made me look for sentences like the ones he doesn't like, and they were all over the place: "His face looked pale and haggard – his manner was hurried and uncertain – and his dress, which I remembered as neat and gentleman like, etc." It also made me look for passages which show sympathy for women and women's rights – of which there are plenty, including one about the heroine being convinced she is under the obligation to marry a man she doesn't love. Her cousin tells her, "Are you to break your heart to set his mind at ease? No man under heaven deserves these sacrifices from us women. Men! They are the enemies of our innocence and our peace – they drag us away from our parents' love and our sisters' friendship – they take us body and soul to themselves, and fasten our helpless lives to theirs as they chain up a dog to his kennel."

I'm up to my ears in this stuff.

Yours
Larry

PS In the copy I read, Collins in a Preface asks reviewers not to tell the story – they should leave "the excitement of surprise." I hope I haven't spoiled it for you if you ever decide to read it.

From: Nicholls@btinternet.com
To: L.Dickerson@verizon.net
13 July 2007

Larry

Thanks. Actually, I read <u>The Woman in White</u> many years ago as a teenager. I won't reread it.

Who was it said you were obsessive?

In sympathy,
Stephen

From: L.Dickerson@verizon.net
To: Nicholls@btinternet.com
July 14, 2007

Dear Stephen

Yeah, that's right. After reading Collins's <u>The Woman in White</u>, I went <u>obsessively</u> looking for the video. I wasn't crazy about the book, so I was hoping to like the movie better. So last night I watched a 1998 video of the story from the BBC. The movie makes awful changes. They have made the most interesting character – Fosco – into a very minor character, and they decided to sex it up by having a maid accuse Hartwright the hero of sexual assault. And Anne Catherick, the Woman in White herself, instead of just dying is thrown off a tower. Just terrible. My advice is, if the book is any good at all, miss the movie if you can. If it's a crummy book, the movie may be an improvement. I'm not exactly saying <u>The Woman in White</u> was a crummy book – just not up to the level of the big guys.

I was <u>really</u> disappointed to find that a 1948 movie of the book with Sidney Greenstreet playing the villain Fosco is not available in video or DVD. When one thinks of all the crap that is available on video, it's a crying shame. Greenstreet is my second favorite old actor – my favorite old actor is everybody else's favorite. Think Maltese Falcon and Casablanca.

Yours
Larry

I know Casablanca by heart. Of all the gin joints. Play it Sam. We'll always have Paris. Don't amount to a hill of beans. The beginning of a beautiful friendship.

Chapter Eleven

From: L.Dickerson@verizon.net
To: Nicholls@btinternet.com
July 20, 2007

Dear Stephen

    Samuel Butler's <u>Erewhon</u> (that's "nowhere" spelled backwards – almost) is the strangest book I've ever read. In class we're reading Butler's big book, <u>The Way of All Flesh</u>, but my gggf writes to Butler about this <u>Erewhon</u> and so I've been reading that one too. <u>Erewhon</u> is really fascinating, but it's not the kind of book you can't put down. You put it down so that you can think about what you've just been reading. You ask yourself, is this just clever silly stuff – or is there something to it? You also laugh out loud in other places. Did you ever read it?

Yours
Larry

From: Nicholls@btinternet.com
To: L.Dickerson@verizon.net
22 July 2007

Larry

No, I have never read <u>Erewhon</u> although I have read <u>The Way of All Flesh</u>.

I know you're just dying to tell me how marvelous <u>Erewhon</u> is.

Stephen

From: L.Dickerson@verizon.net
To: Nicholls@btinternet.com
July 23, 2007

   Are you getting a little jumpy about my long emails?

From: Nicholls@btinternet.com
To: L.Dickerson@verizon.net
25 July 2007

Not really. Fire away.

From: L.Dickerson@verizon.net
To: Nicholls@btinternet.com
27 July 2007

   Okay. A traveler named Higgs gets lost in the wilds of New Zealand and stumbles into a lost civilization called "Erewhon." Their laws and their whole viewpoint (maybe their "Weltanschauung"?) are really weird. For example, back about four hundred years ago, the Erewhonians destroyed all mechanical things. The only machinery to be seen anywhere is in a museum that has on display parts of old steam engines and clocks. The Erewhonians were big on evolution, and they got worried that there was no telling when machines at the rate they were going on evolving (and getting smaller) would take over from humans. Does that sound familiar? Computers? Do you remember

IBM's Deep Blue beating that brat Bobby Fischer at chess? Or was it the Russian guy? In any case Butler is writing this in 1870.

Also in the past, the Erewhonians nearly became complete vegetarians. You could eat only animals that died a "natural death" or were still-born. You could also eat animals who "committed suicide." And of course the "rates of suicide" among pigs and cows and sheep shot way up. And you could only eat spoiled eggs because eating a fresh egg was destroying a <u>potential</u> chicken. Sound familiar? And people decided, again with the help of evolution, that plants were "cousins" to animals and so that it was wrong to eat any plants except those what again died a "natural death" – like fruit that fell from trees and was laying on the ground and about to rot. The country was starving to death until good old fashioned common sense took over in the diet department.

But they still have plenty of strange beliefs. The craziest is that the only crimes are misfortune – bad luck, bad health, and bad looks. What we think of as crimes, like embezzling money, are treated the way we treat sickness. The embezzler gets treatment by a "straightener" – just as we would send a sick man to a doctor. And friends come and visit him to cheer him up. In a little while the straightener will straighten out this little wrinkle in his personality (in this case a taste for stealing), and he will soon be back to his place in society with no bad effects to his reputation.

But to get sick, or to have bad luck, that's criminal. Higgs attends the court trial of a young man accused of consumption. The young man's defense lawyer does his best, by claiming that his client had only been making believe he had consumption in order to cheat the insurance company – but it doesn't work. The judge gives a long charge to the jury about this "radically vicious" young man. The poor fellow has a long list of prior convictions for "aggravated bronchitis" and has been imprisoned many times for illnesses over his short life. The judge says, "You may say that it is your misfortune to be criminal; I answer that it is your crime to be unfortunate." The poor guy gets life in prison, with hard labor, and soon dies.

Now this sounds horrible to the reader. But Higgs, in spite of all his disgust at what he has seen at the trial, thinks it through and puts down some second thoughts. Life itself seems to punish people for their misfortunes. Nature, in evolution, certainly bears down hard on the

unlucky and the sick. At the same time, Nature rewards the lucky —
namely those who by chance inherit changes that make them more fit
to survive. And we ourselves go around praising and rewarding people
for their good fortune. You never know where Butler stands, and that is
where my gggf's letters come in. I send you some transcriptions:

Paternoster Row
London. E.C.

15 November 1872

Dear Mr Butler

    May I congratulate you on <u>Erewhon</u>. *It is a first novel like none
other in our day. It's a kind of Utopia (or reverse Utopia); and it is in
the company of* <u>Robinson Crusoe</u> *and* <u>Gulliver's Travels</u>, *and
certainly will become in my view a classic in its own right and
deserve to stand side by side with these two great works of English
literature.*
    *I don't write only to congratulate you; I have an ulterior motive.
For some dozen years now I have been writing to our leading
novelists. I understand that you consider yourself a "prose man," and
if you don't mind the company, I'd like to say that my predilections
also lie with prose. Of course there's Shakespeare (and a few others)
who give us prose people pause, but he was of course a special case. I
have been writing to our novelists and trying to get them to give me
their opinions on themes they develop, saying where they stand on
certain issues, or, if not where they stand, then where a particular
novel itself "stands."*
    *The thing that most intrigues me in your book — amongst many
other excellent things, like the "College of Unreason," etc — is the
"Musical Banks" chapter. If I take your meaning rightly, you are one
of the honestest writers going these days, more honest, almost, than
Charles Darwin himself, who seems sometimes to be tiptoeing
around a question that people keep asking in relation to him: does
he believe there is anything au fond to religion? Or is there at bottom
nothing supporting its currency, to use your own terms. I promise not*

〉 *143* 〈

to advertise your response to these musings. Anything you say to me will be strictly private and will stay that way.

I have also been asking our novelists what they think of the novels of their fellow writers. George Eliot has recently given us Middlemarch. Have you read it?

Do pardon this old bookseller's pesky letter and forgive the intrusion, but I'd count it a privilege to hear from the latest leading novelist to enter the lists – I say this as a bookseller and as a reader.

Yours sincerely
Jeremy MacDowell

⌒

15, Cliffords Inn
London. E.C.
Nov. 18, 1872

Dear Mr MacDowell

Thank you for your kind words about Erewhon. As for where the author of Erewhon stands, I must leave that to the reader to deduce for himself.
As for prose and Shakespeare, I am given to saying that Shakespeare is as good as prose. I mean someday to write a book on Shakespeare's sonnets. There has been a lot of drivel published on that score, and I hope to sort the whole thing out – at least to my own satisfaction.

Yours truly
S. Butler

I read about half of Middlemarch and hated it.

⌒

21 November 1872

Dear Mr Butler

Thank you for your prompt response to my importunate letter. Thanks too for your harsh but frank expression of your feelings about Middlemarch. I myself find that in places it seems a bit laboured, but masterful nonetheless. Still, I prefer Adam Bede and The Mill on the Floss.

You say, and with more than adequate correctness, that the work must speak for itself. I readily concede the point. But you can perhaps sympathise with a reader who wonders if he is in fact reading the work "correctly," that is to say, reading it, interpreting it, in a way that is in line with what the author has intended to say, or how he intended it to be interpreted.

Yours sincerely
Jeremy MacDowell

But Butler is stubborn and won't tell him anything about what Erewhon "means" and won't get into any talk about the merits of George Eliot's novels. So, let's skip up 25 years and my gggf – by now retired – is still writing to him. They have become good enough friends to be on that last name basis. My gggf writes, first, to say that he has just finished Butler's latest book The Authoress of the Odyssey (Butler could use "authoress," but not me), telling him the book showed enormous knowledge of the field but saying he doubted anyone will believe him that a woman wrote the Odyssey. Second, he wants Butler to tell him "exactly and precisely" how he – Butler – differs from Darwin on evolution:

15, Cliffords Inn
London. E.C.
Dec. 4, 1897

Dear MacDowell

Thirty publishers turned down the <u>Authoress of the Odyssey</u> before I published it at my own expense with Longman. No doubt it will now be dismissed by thirty reviewers incapable of judging the material. You I excuse on no particular grounds. As for my differences with Darwin, I have neither time nor inclination to rehearse my differences with that man. I could tell you to read two or three books of mine on the subject, but I forego doing so to an old friend who has never done me any harm, especially as you seem to have read most of everything else I have perpetrated. Young Bernard Shaw agrees with me on evolution, if that does you any good. Don't mean to be abrupt, and I do appreciate your continued praise for my (other) writings. But please don't get me wrong. Just because I firmly embrace evolution (my own kind of evolution) and because I see organised religion as all astray and usually doing more harm than good, that doesn't mean that I think the scientists, or so-called scientists, or self-satisfied agnostics or certain <u>dogmatic atheists</u> have it right, either. Any deeply held conviction is wrong except the conviction that deeply held convictions are all wrong.

Always yours
S. Butler

Nelson Road
Whitstable, Kent

6 December 1897

Dear Butler

Just one moment, my friend. Why do you call me a "dogmatic" atheist? Just because I won't believe in something I can't see and can find no evidence for and certainly no proof for – does that make me "dogmatic"?

Yours always
Jeremy MacDowell

⌒

15, Cliffords Inn
London. E.C.
Dec. 8th, 1897

Dear MacDowell

My dear bookseller-turned-philosopher, I can only say what I believe to be the case in your case.

Yrs truly
S. Butler

Just remember that Tennyson tells us that there are more things wrought by prayer than this world dreams of, but he doesn't say if they are good things or bad things.

⌒

Nelson Road
Whitstable, Kent

10 December 1897

Dear Butler

　Your Tennyson is very good, but you avoid my question.

JM

15, Cliffords Inn
London. E.C.
Dec. 12, 1897

Dear MacDowell

　I've lost track of the question. On the subject of losing, Tennyson says it is better to have loved and lost than never to have loved at all, while I say that it is better to have loved and lost than never to have lost at all.
　Beyond this I won't go, just as earlier in our correspondence I would not enter into your irreverence toward established religion. My own impieties are the only ones I countenance. I'll only go so far, even in thought. For example, I can envision St. Paul smoking a cigarette, but I cannot imagine Jesus himself smoking.

Yrs truly
S. Butler

Nelson Road
Whitstable, Kent

15 December 1897

Dear Butler

    That Tennyson is equally good — but the cigarette smoking is even better. I see Tennyson is not your favourite. But don't you like his line "There lives more faith in honest doubt"?

              Yours always
              Jeremy MacDowell

15, Cliffords Inn
London. E.C.
Dec. 17, 1897

Deur MacDowell

    No, I don't like it. I prefer "There lives more doubt in honest faith."

              Yrs
              S. Butler

How do you like them apples? Your pal Leonard Hill gave me such a long answer on evolution "vis a vis" my novelists that I feel that I could answer my gggf's question on Butler differing with Darwin. Namely, Butler believed in this "unconscious memory" junk. (Whenever somebody tells me I have an "unconscious" motive for what I'm doing, I tell him he's talking through his hat.) Butler thought that over millions of years we have inherited "unconscious memories," including a shaky belief in some kind of supreme being. But it's not just us who do the remembering. Everything in the universe is made up of one big "life force" that somehow or other "remembers" — I forget exactly what it is that <u>things</u> remember. When I heard this, I was reminded of hearing some famous classical singer talking on the radio and saying that Carnegie Hall was such a special sounding place because so many famous singers and musicians had performed there. Their sound waves bounced off the walls and woodwork, and the walls and the woodwork <u>remembered</u> these sounds. And that was why Carnegie Hall was such a great sounding space. Sounds crackpot to me.

Yours
Larry

Butler's father (who he hated) was a clergyman, and he told Sammy that this book <u>Erewhon</u> killed his mother – which I doubt. Women are tougher than that, don't you think? The part that was supposed to have killed his mother was the "Musical Banks" chapter – the very one my gggf asked Butler about. This chapter tells how in the capital city there's a huge old bank set back on a piazza. It reminds you of the distant past. Inside are huge pillars and stained glass windows and a handful of tourists walking around. The tellers give people (mostly all women) Musical Bank notes in exchange for commercial bank money. Everyone knows that the Musical Bank money is worthless. It's toy money, but everyone makes believe it's really more important than commercial money.

<u>Please</u> read the entire chapter. I'll mail you a xeroxed copy.

From: Nicholls@btinternet.com
To: L.Dickerson@verizon.net
29 July 2007

Dear Larry

I'm becoming habituated to expecting the MacDowell letters to be engaging, and these letters to and from Butler are no exception. And your powers of description are coming along very nicely.

There is no need to send me the chapter. I have anticipated you. I'm a member of a remarkable institution, the London Library – a private subscription library (you pay a membership fee) – from which you can borrow books, and I took out a copy of Erewhon and will read the whole thing some evening (as you know, it's not a long book), taking special note of that Musical Banks chapter. All "in due course," as you love to hear me say. I see from the introduction to the book that in the sequel, Erewhon Revisited, your friend Higgs comes back to Erewhon, after having escaped thirty years earlier in a hot air balloon, only to find that he has been made into a god who ascended into heaven. A whole new religion, Sunchildism, has arisen, and legend has changed the balloon into a horse-drawn chariot. This new religion has its own relics, like dung from the horses who drew the chariot into heaven. Don't tell me, I know that you know what Butler is doing here.

Your explanation of "unconscious memory" (of which I had never heard) reminded me of Byron making fun of Coleridge for having taken to "explaining metaphysics to the nation / I wish he would explain his explanation." And never mind who Coleridge was, if the name means little to you. As you would say, you get the idea. We can leave unconscious memory where you left it – an absurdity. Although, now I think of it, the famous psychologist Carl Jung held for the existence of "archetypes" existing in the inherited "collective unconscious" of humans.

Best
Stephen

I'm off on holiday for two weeks to the Greek islands. Will resume our email conversation after 18 August.

From: L.Dickerson@verizon.net
To: Nicholls@btinternet.com
July 30, 2007

Dear Stephen,

Have a good vacation. I understand all Englishmen who can afford it go to someplace in the summer to get some sun. I won't be pestering you with questions for a while.

I'm sorry I mentioned unconscious memory.

Sounds like as if <u>Erewhon</u> didn't kill his mother, the <u>Revisited</u> one would have. But she was already dead.

There's so much to read. At times I feel a little snowed under.

Have a safe trip.

Yours
Larry

From: Nicholls@btinternet.com
To: L.Dickerson@verizon.net
20 August 2007

Dear Larry

I'm back at work and also back on my email, and I can only say, as the expression goes, easy does it. As you know, "Art is long." I repeat yet again my advice to read only the books mentioned either by your great-great-grandfather or by his correspondents. That's plenty, and even this reading should remain secondary to your work on the transcriptions themselves.

As I told you, at your insistent urging, I got hold of a copy of <u>Erewhon</u>. Thanks for insisting. I am especially taken with the chapter on the College of Unreason. This place is obviously a combination of Oxford and Cambridge. Its Professors of Inconsistency and Professors of Evasion, with their miraculous talent for gracefully sitting on the fence, are good fun. I laughed at the place where a professor gets into trouble for trying to add a new adverb to the utterly useless "Hypothetical Language" (Butler's joke on the predominance of the study of Greek in English schools and universities in his day). I was struck too by his saying that university students don't suffer much at the hands of their professors because they don't pay them any attention. The real good that a university education does for students comes from the beauty of the college buildings, gardens, and walks; these things, Butler says, have a "hallowing" and refining influence on young people. That's very nicely observed.

Butler is so contrarian, so anti-intuitive, as to sound almost postmodern. Please don't ask me what "postmodernism" is, as I have, floating in the back of my mind, only the vaguest sense of what the word means.

Are we nearly there?

Best
Stephen

From: L.Dickerson@verizon.net
To: Nicholls@btinternet.com
Aug. 22, 2007

Stephen

   Welcome home.
   I'm making very good progress. Patience, my friend.

                                        Larry

Chapter Twelve

From: L.Dickerson@verizon.net
To: Nicholls@btinternet.com
Sept. 2, 2007

Dear Stephen

I'm sort of nearing the finish line, and I'm sending you a run of my transcribed Thackeray letters. These letters are the earliest of all. They start about three months earlier than the first ones with Dickens. Me sending these late is a little ass backwards, but you'll see why, I think. Remember that I already sent you one Thackeray letter about Trollope. Regular mutual admiration society those two.

Also, at long last I am finally getting around to sending you some of the Thackeray drawings – <u>photographs</u> of them, not tracings. These drawings are at the bottom of letters after the signature. The captions are by Thackeray. It's sort of like he signs his name twice.

I'm also giving you my gggf's side, because he has plenty to say in this case. The two men met, just like with Dickens, through Robert Bell, who invited my gggf to join him and others at the same Garrick Club. Notice how quickly Thackeray and my gggf move to a last name basis.

At first I was a little confused reading these letters, because I thought a snob was somebody who looks down on people who have less than he has – like less money, a smaller house, a lousier job, etc. But I see that for Thackeray it also worked in the other direction too. A snob is especially someone who <u>sucks up</u> and bows down to people with more money, power, importance, etc, than himself. Once you have that straight, these letters and <u>Vanity Fair</u> make much more sense.

You'll see that my gggf doesn't try to conceal the fact that he thinks

Thackeray never wrote anything like <u>Vanity Fair</u> again. In one of his "Reading" notes my gggf writes, "WMT, they say, has for years been much taken up by society people, and it has worked against his gift. No doubt this may very well be true. But I think that to have written that one novel was enough. It actually makes me look at human nature in a different – and hardly better – light."

Here goes – without commercial interruption, as they say. Tell me what you think.

Paternoster Row
London. E.C.

12 February 1861

Dear Mr Thackeray

It was a pleasure and a privilege to have met you through the good offices of my good friend Robert Bell. It seems that everyone likes Robert Bell. He is a very generous man and very kind to fellow writers and journalists, and even to booksellers, like myself. I expect you feel the same way about Bell.

Yours very truly
Jeremy MacDowell

I can't remember when I last had such good talk, at once so light and entertaining and yet so instructive.

36 Onslow Square,
Brompton

13 February 1861

Dear MacDowell

It was also enjoyable for your humble servant to meet you. I

understand you are a bookseller who knows what he is doing.
Always happy to meet a good man who also sells books. That in
itself makes us colleagues because I am in the book writing business
and we scribblers write our books to be sold. We write, as Dr
Johnson said, for money, else we are blockheads.

As for Bob Bell, I subscribe precisely to your sentiments. He is
indeed a princely figure, though of course we mustn't tell him so.

Yes, the Garrick is sometimes the locus for capital talk. One turn
of our conversation yesternight stayed with me. That was the
discussion of some writers falling off in later years and never
equaling their earlier work. Wordsworth was one obvious example,
but others came to mind. Of course we did not speak of any present
company, but I couldn't help but think of myself. Everyone believes,
though nobody will say so to me, that I have seldom come up to the
promise of Vanity Fair. *One does what one can.*

Your Obedient Servant etc
Wm M Thackeray

Paternoster Row
London. E.C.

15 February 1861

Dear Thackeray

I remember the conversation very well, and, truth to say, I also
thought of you but not in the disappointed and disappointing way
you may think. My thought was that if one's early work is non-pareil,
if there is nothing like it, then how could *one go on topping (or even*
keeping up with) that? An impossibility. I'll make this confession to
you and trust that you will not think a friend of Robert Bell could be
praising your work fulsomely. Vanity Fair, *which I have read and*
re-read half a dozen times, changed my view of human nature and,

in fact, though this is only logical, changed my view of my very self. That's the kind of thing one could not tell a person to his face.

Yours very truly
Jeremy MacDowell

⌐

36 Onslow Square,
Brompton

16 February 1861

My dear MacDowell

Merciful powers! I hat, my dear Sir, is prodigiously high praise. And if, as you say, you had told me this to my face, I would have been embarrassed and maybe even have cut you. On the other hand, you don't say whether the book affected you for better or for worse. Perhaps I shouldn't ask.

Yrs
WMT

⌐

Paternoster Row
London. E.C.

18 February 1861

Dear Thackeray

Again in the sort of thing that gentlemen are usually shy of doing – and with an exactitude that would be impossible in conversation – I will beg your pardon as I write out a few lines from places in the novel (I have the book open before me) that epitomise what affected me so greatly.

If I am trying your patience, just skip to my signature and accept my sincere thanks for writing this book.

For example, there's old Miss Crawley with her 30,000 pounds to leave in her will to her nephews: "What a dignity it gives an old Lady, that balance at the bankers! How tenderly we look at her faults, what a kind good-natured old creature we find her!"

And then there's that delightful old wretch her brother, Sir Pitt Crawley, crude, penny-pinching, and debauched, that "philosopher with a taste for the low life," to whom people bow down because he is a baronet:

> Vanity Fair – Vanity Fair! Here was a man who could not spell, and did not care to read – who had the habits and cunning of a boor: whose aim in life was pettifogging: who never had a taste, or emotion, or enjoyment, but what was sordid and foul; and yet he had rank and honours, and power, somehow; and was a dignitary of the state. He was a high sheriff, and rode in a golden coach. Great ministers and statesmen courted him; and in Vanity Fair he had a higher place than the most brilliant genius or spotless virtue.

And, famously, there's that "little sinner" Becky Sharp protesting she could be a good woman on five thousand pounds a year, and you commenting, "And who knows but Rebecca was right – and that it is only a question of money and fortune which made the difference between her and an honest woman? If you take temptations into account, who is to say that he is better than his neighbor? An Alderman coming home from a turtle feast will not step out of his carriage and steal a leg of mutton; but put him to starve, and see if he will not purloin a loaf."

Ah, but this is useless. Silly of me to try. A few quoted lines from here and there cannot do justice to the effect that the entire book has on one. It's wondrously comic, satiric, and above all morally clarifying and enlightening about just what we are – all of us, this reader very particularly – namely, "practitioners in Vanity Fair."

Yours very truly
Jeremy MacDowell

36 Onslow Square,
Brompton

19 Feb 1861

My dear MacDowell

Ye gods what man can resist such praise? May you live 1000 years. And talk of patience, what's to be made of yours – in writing these lines out for me? If you told me you had them by heart, I would put you down for a prevaricator, a good-hearted one, but a liar nonetheless.

It's a peculiar feeling for me, reading over passages written out by the hand of another – passages I hurriedly put down on paper twenty years ago. So much water has gone under the bridge since then, but no matter, it is somehow bracing – and I needs bracing I does – to read that which someone says he has found affecting, things I dashed off with the little printer's devil waiting at the door for copy.

But, by the bye, something you have written reminds me of a little correspondence I once had with my delightful friend George Lewes. It's funny, or rather not so funny, the things one remembers from out of the many things one should remember. Lewes was – long before I knew him – a public apologist for my writings. But, strangely enough, for all his praise of my scribblings way back then in the 1840s, he was upset, and said so in print, by this very passage about Becky Sharp being right about how she could be good if she were rich and the example I offered of the Alderman coming home from a feast and not being tempted to steal a leg of mutton. For Lewes this was as much as saying that honesty is "only the virtue of abundance." This, he said, was "deep misanthropy" on my part. On reading this, I wrote to him – violating the law Thou Shalt Not Answer Thy Critics – because of his general goodwill towards my stuff. I tried to defend myself by saying that the passage was meant only as a warning to anyone well placed and comfortable in the

world, anyone reasonably well behaved and satisfied with himself,
lest he should be decorously angry at the errors of less lucky men. I
admitted that a refrain of roguery runs through the Vanity Fair story;
and I admitted that the world was not altogether like the one there
depicted – though a lot more like it than we like to own. The story is
sung in a minor key, with only occasional nods towards brighter
things – the kinds of things I myself dare not preach.

Your Obedient Servant
Wm M Thackeray

Although I frequently forget where I put my slippers, my visual
memory is good, and here's the misanthropic showman of Vanity
Fair as I drew myself those many long years ago.

Paternoster Row
London. E.C.

19 Feb 1861

My dear Thackeray

I trust Lewes has since seen the error of his ways. I shall treasure
the drawing.
Since I am a garrulous correspondent, I'll declare this: <u>Vanity Fair</u>
taught me not only that I am a practitioner in Vanity Fair but that,

more specifically (although I would probably have denied it even to myself), I am a snob. However, since you demonstrate that just about everybody else is also a snob, I don't feel too bad about it. In fact I feel rather smugly superior to other people because I now know the truth about myself in this regard, and this in turn gives me an advantage over those who do not know this truth about themselves. How Socratic of me.

I cannot help but be impressed by nobility, success, fame, money. I confess to being a snob even in my eagerness to meet and talk with you. If Lord So-and-So deigns to speak with me, I am quite pleased. Just the nod of the royal head would send me (and most of us) into ecstasies. With Englishmen, social position is more important than money — unlike in America, where I understand money is everything. Were I to meet Lord Palmerston tomorrow, I would not discount my pleasure just because many of his policies are abhorrent to me. He is Prime Minister of England, and that is so grand a thing that I would be delighted to meet him. I am rambling on In a spirit of elation because I have the ear (though I may soon lose it) of the man who awakened in me a self-knowledge that still startles me.

As for calling your work cynical, as some shallow people have done, I say that if cynicism means looking the facts in the face, then you stand accused and condemned as charged. Human nature, as Sydney Smith famously said, is a sorry business at the best, and one shouldn't expect too much from it. As for the accusation that you are on the Devil's side without knowing it, like Milton with his Satan; that you are, to wit, a secret admirer of Becky Sharp and that your expressed fondness for that nonentity Amelia Sedley is all ironic — what are we to do with people who wouldn't know an irony if it jumped up and bit them?

I had better cease now or you'll accuse me of descending into what you brand "humbug."

Yours very truly
Jeremy MacDowell

36 Onslow Square,
Brompton

21 Feb 1861

My dear MacDowell

Mon Dieu your kind words leave me speechless. Dammy, I cannot agree with you without seeming smug and to disagree would be disingenuous. I am of course aware of the criticism of <u>Vanity Fair</u> and its author – most authors are excessively aware of what is said of them in the papers. And naturally enough, the nasty stuff always sticks in the mind. Ten good reviews (I speak hypothetically of course) are weighed down by one bad notice. C'est la vie. I have been called heartless, cynical, morose, bitter, and misanthropic for so long that I am helplessly pleased when anyone finds out that my heart is not altogether stone, that in fact that particular organ of mine is filled with anything but unkindness even towards those &c &c.

"Socratic" indeed. More to the point, when I loikes a man, I loikes him, and I'd loike you to kyindly come dine with me for an humble meal at the Garrick on Thursday 28th. I'll ask two other gentlemen and our evening will be passed in philosophical converse.

Pax vobiscum
Wm M Thackeray

I am overjoyed to be mentioned in the same sentence with that cleric extraordinaire, the late Sydney Smith, the wittiest man in England, and one of the shrewdest. But don't overwhelm me with laudations or I shall drown in them.

WMT making a long face after one bad review

Paternoster Row
London. E.C.

21 Feb 1861

My dear Thackeray

  Will be delighted for Thursday.
  We are two complainers, aren't we, lamenting the sad business
that is human nature. What to do? I don't expect an answer.

Yours truly
Jeremy MacDowell

36 Onslow Square,
Brompton

23 Feb 1861

My dear MacDowell

  Here's an answer anyway. What to do? For one thing 'tis best not
to think too much about it. But if we must think about it, I suppose
we ought sometimes to remind our old complaining selves that
success and fame really _are_ luck. Indeed that even good behaviour is
a matter of luck, as in those words of that little scamp Becky Sharp.
What else to do? If I can become a preacher for the nonce, we should
try to do as little harm as possible; make the best of private
attachments to family and friends; and take as much pleasure as we
can from the good things of the earth like wine and food – decent
claret, bouillabaisse &c – and (in our higher moments) from the
various arts. That ain't the Ten Beatitudes or the Sermon on the
Mount (or are they the same thing?), but it's the best I can do.
Enough – more than enough of my twaddling on there anent.

Yr preacher manqué
WMThackeray

PS   Nowadays nobody ever mentions my last big novel, <u>The Virginians</u>. That is because no living person has ever gotten through it. It nearly killed me. If you say anything good about it, I'll never speak to you again.

WMT indulging in thoughts of the good things of the world

WMT on hearing someone praise <u>The Virginians</u>.

I've given you in advance these Thackeray transcriptions because I have come to be a great fan of <u>Vanity Fair</u> and couldn't wait for you to see some of these letters.

Of course not everyone liked Thackeray. I've just read that that Thomas Carlyle – you mentioned him to me long ago as an important Scotsman – thought Thackeray had more talent than Dickens, but at the same time he says that Thackeray "had no conviction except that a man ought to be a gentleman, and ought not to be a snob. This was about the sum of belief that was in him." He also said that for Thackeray "the test of greatness in a man was whether he (Thackeray) would like to meet him at a tea-party."

I am on my second time round through <u>Vanity Fair</u> and am enjoying it even more this time. Like a snob, I am very pleased with myself for liking this famous book.

Yours
Larry

From: Nicholls@btinternet.com
To: L.Dickerson@verizon.net
6 September 2007

Dear Larry

I can see why these Thackeray letters are your favourites. And the "self-portrait" sketches are a very lively complement. It's pretty clear that Thackeray is by now your preferred reading among your Victorians.

Best
Stephen

-

From: L.Dickerson@verizon.net
To: Nicholls@btinternet.com
Sept. 8, 2007

Dear Stephen,

Yeah, you got that one right. As I told you, I'm into rereading Vanity Fair. And this is in spite of it being 800 pages long. I find I'm in very good company in thinking this is a very special book. This includes many famous people I never heard of like G. K. Chesterton, Edith Wharton, Max Beerbohm, Joyce Cary et al.

And Irving Gross, who is himself no ham and egger in this business, feels the same way about Vanity Fair as these people and yours truly feel about it. (I've been sitting in on Gross's summer version of the same course — he does it sort of different every time.) I can see that he is pleased that some of us in his class agree with him about Vanity Fair. Gross says he has a "hobby horse" of trying to convince people that really great comedy is as good as really great tragedy — or even better, because it's more rare. He quotes James Joyce to prove his point. I forget exactly what it was this James Joyce said, but I get the point. Gross says Vanity Fair is "the English War and Peace." And that people who are annoyed with this kind of statement don't appreciate the greatness of great comedy. They think things have to be sad or depressing to be important. Why can't we say that <u>War and Peace</u> (which of course I've never read) is the Russian <u>Vanity Fair</u>? And, for the record, <u>Vanity Fair</u> was written first.

Yours
Larry

Just a bit more, and it's going from the sublime to the ridiculous, as they say. Last night I rented the movie of <u>Vanity Fair</u> with Reese Witherspoon. Now I <u>know</u> that the movie, as I've said before, is not going to be the book, but, Jesus, this is awful. It's overacted, the story is all changed, and there's a silly happy ending. Okay, I know you can't take an 800 page book and just boil it down to a two hour movie, but this one is really terrible. Maybe for someone who doesn't know the book – like I didn't until a few months ago – maybe it's okay for them. To such a person the movie might not be half bad. What did I expect? Gross says – and who am I to doubt him – that the whole book "turns" on the one telling the story, the "narrator," and that his "voice" is there on every page – and of course a movie can't have a narrator. Except for voice over stuff, of which there is none in this movie. I regard the two hours spent looking at this video of <u>Vanity Fair</u> as time just thrown away and shot to hell. I kept thinking it would get better but it got worser. I mean worse – that old New Jersey background.

I've learned that the audio tape of the unabridged <u>Vanity Fair</u> runs 40 hours. If life wasn't so short or if I had a <u>very</u> long drive to make, I'd think about renting the tapes (24 of them) and soaking it in. Or soaking in it.

Gross claims he knows a dentist who rereads <u>Vanity Fair</u> every year, just to give himself a different perspective.

From: Nicholls@btinternet.com
To: L.Dickerson@verizon.net
9 September 2007

Larry

Sounds as though you have become a real Thackerayan. I'll avoid the movie.

Does all this mean you are about to "deliver"? Don't you think it is about time?

Stephen

PS I have never heard the term "ham and egger."

⌒

From: L.Dickerson@verizon.net
To: Nicholls@btinternet.com
Sept. 10, 2007

Stephen

　　Yes I'm getting nearer and nearer to that finish line. Courage, my friend.
　　Ham and egger – can't you guess? An amateur.

Larry

⌒

From: Nicholls@btinternet.com
To: L.Dickerson@verizon.net
11 September 2007

I didn't say I couldn't figure out what it meant. I said I hadn't heard the term.

⌒

From: L.Dickerson@verizon.net
To: Nicholls@btinternet.com
Sept. 12, 2007

Stephen

Christ, you've got me there.

Larry

PS Did you know that if Thackeray's daughter Minnie had not died, Thackeray would have been the grandfather of that famous Virginia Woolf? I myself don't know or care a damn about Virginia Woolf – she's not in my century. I knew about the movie "Who's Afraid of Virginia Woolf" about a drunken married couple. It starred Richard Burton and Elizabeth Taylor and came out way back in the 1960s. And just for the hell of it, I rented the video – for the Thackeray connection. The cover says the picture won five academy awards. It's powerful stuff but depressing as hell. The whole thing reminded me of the story of the fellow who says that when he goes to the movies, he goes to get entertained, he doesn't go to the movies to see a lot of hollering and screaming and adultery and sodomy – "I get all I want of that at home," he says.
    Alright, don't correct me. I looked carefully at the video box and the movie is from a play, and the name is just a running joke on Who's afraid of the big bad wolf. It's not by Virginia Woolf at all. We live and

learn. At least my record stays perfect, and I can still say I don't know anything about any book by Virginia Woolf. (Two o's in the name – at least I got that straight.) Besides, I don't have time, with reading all these Victorian novels and doing my research. And besides that, I must admit it's a slim connection between Thackeray and Virginia Woolf almost being his granddaughter. Thackeray's daughter Minnie Thackeray married a writer named Leslie Stephen but died after half a dozen years. Then Stephen married again, and his second wife became the mother of Virginia Stephen Woolf.

From: Nicholls@btinternet.com
To: L.Dickerson@verizon.net
14 September 2007

Come on, you're either kidding me or being very naive. I presume it's the first. You know heredity doesn't work that way. If Stephen's first wife (Thackeray's daughter) hadn't died and they'd had a daughter, she wouldn't have been Virginia Woolf. But you are joshing me.

From: L.Dickerson@verizon.net
To: Nicholls@btinternet.com
Sept. 16, 2007

Dear Stephen

I'm not saying which it is.
But I did at first think the movie was from a novel by Virginia Woolf. It was two hours of really rough drunk talk. The cover box says the movie broke "taboos about subjects and indecent language." Christ, I believe it. In movies today every other word is fuck this and fuck that. If this Virginia Woolf movie broke the taboos about bad language,

I frankly don't know if that's a good thing or a bad thing. Hell, you yourself know I'm not stuffy about bad language but I think you can overdo it.

Back to my real work.

Yours
Larry

Chapter Thirteen

From: L.Dickerson@verizon.net
To: L.Hill@lincoln.ox.ac.uk
Sept. 21, 2007

Dear Leonard Hill

I haven't troubled you for months, and this is <u>positively</u> the last time. I'm coming down the homestretch. The work for my book is nearing the end. I'll try to couch the questions so you can give me a short answer. I'm doing Thomas Hardy and especially <u>Tess of the D'Urbervilles</u>.

1/ I'll be really disappointed if you tell me I got this one all wrong. Some of Hardy's critics say he is "an unreclaimed determinist" and that he likes to put this idea into novels like <u>Tess of the D'Urbervilles</u>. My question is do I have this straight? "Religious determinism" means that the creator has determined that you are going to heaven or hell, and there is nothing you can do about it. If you're a sinner but predestined for heaven, you'll have a deathbed conversion and fly up to Jesus. If you're a saint living a holy life but predestined for hell, you'll turn around just as you're dying and do something terrible and you join the devil in hell forever – though how a dying saint could manage to commit a serious sin on his deathbed is unclear to me. It's probably clearer to religious people, of which I'm not one. To me the whole idea of heaven and hell is pure malarkey.

But "moral determinism" is what they bring against Hardy. (They couldn't accuse him of religious determinism because he wasn't a religious believer.) This moral determinism holds that everything we do is determined by our background – our genetic makeup and all our "interactions with our environment." Nature and nurture. So if at age twenty nine I choose to buy a green car instead of a red car, or to shoot a man instead of not shooting him, my act is predetermined. It's been determined by millions of interactions that my particular set of genes have had with my particular environment all these years, including my nine months in the womb. Result, no free will. I <u>think</u> I have free will, but that's only because I have been brought up – predetermined – to believe I have it. I can't help myself believing it. On the other hand, in a case where a person <u>does</u> doubt free will, determinism would mean that he can't help doubting it – his whole background, nature and nurture, adds up to him not being able to help himself from doubting it.

2/ The passage in <u>Tess</u> about the "ache of modernism" – I figure this means that in modern times people think too much and know too much (like as for example it being a godless universe without a purpose), and that thoughts like these can make your mind ache.

3/ What do you think of T. S. Eliot (no relation to "my" George Eliot, of course, though both with one "l") saying, as I read somewhere, that Hardy's style "touches the sublime and without having passed through the stage of good."

Thanks
Larry Dickerson

⌣⌐

From: L.Hill@lincoln.ox.ac.uk
To: L.Dickerson@verizon.net
25 September 2007

Dear Larry Dickerson

1/ Sounds good to me.

2/ Ditto.

3/ That's a famous remark by TSE about Hardy's prose being sublime without being good. For one thing, Hardy was chiefly self-taught. And some critics think this crops up not just in his so often demonstrating to us how much he knows about the Greek and Roman classics, but especially, and more damagingly, in his overuse of abstract language. These critics think that Hardy can't help showing off all the big abstract – one could say even pretentious – words that he knows. And writers of fiction are supposed to be on their guard against excessive use of abstract words. I expect that if you took an adult education course in fiction writing, you would be told to keep your language concrete and specific. Not "He expressed his gratitude with countless expressions of indebtedness," but "He said 'Thank you' five times." Not "His age reached antediluvian even prelapsarian proportions," but "He was 103." The words "gratitude," "expressions," and "indebtedness" are abstract; the phrase "antediluvian even prelapsarian proportions" is unspecific and abstract, and vague – not to mention ostentatious.

So I open the book you are working with, Tess of the D'Urbervilles, and turn to an early and important passage (a favourite passage of mine) – where Tess is driving her father's horse cart and has an accident that kills the horse. There's great specificity: The other cart's shaft has driven into her horse's breast "like a sword, and from the wound his life's blood was spouting in a stream, and falling with a hiss into the road." This is followed by what some think of as overblown language: "The huge pool of blood was already assuming the iridescence of coagulation; and when the sun rose a million prismatic hues were reflected from it." It's not that there's anything wrong with words like "iridescence" and "coagulation" – only the question of their suitability here. And, mind, there are plenty of readers who admire everything in Hardy and who are not the least troubled by his occasional grand language.

For those who do fault the recherché and abstract language, the question arises: how is it that even for these critics Hardy is one of the greatest of novelists? One explanation is that Hardy is such an extraordinary poet in prose that he casts over the entire story so mesmerising a spell that the sporadic over-the-top language doesn't matter. A great novel succeeds in spite of faults.

Yours cordially
L. Hill

I look forward to seeing your book in print.

⌒

From: L.Dickerson@verizon.net
To: L.Hill@lincoln.ox.ac.uk
Sept. 27, 2007

Dear Leonard Hill

    As per usual you have helped me greatly. I see what you mean. Never gave any thought to the difference between abstract and concrete language.
    I won't even make you read a long letter of five thank yous.

Thank you
Larry Dickerson

    You'll be first after Stephen to receive a copy of my book.

⌒

From: L.Dickerson@verizon.net
To: Nicholls@btinternet.com
Sept. 27, 2007

Dear Stephen

    I am really moving along fast now. Just knocked off Hardy, and I'm a regular expert on "determinism" and Hardy's sometimes "overblown" style. I'm not letting on who helped me.

Now here's a late letter from Hardy to my gggf that I think you'll like:

Max Gate
Dorchester

December 3, 1896

My dear MacDowell

Thank you for criticising the critics of Tess and Jude — although by now all that seems long ago. Such sagacious youths they were, my reviewers:

Half of them say my early novels are best.

The other half says my later novels are best.

Still others say my novels are good in character but bad in plot.

A nearly equal number say the novels are good in plot but bad in character.

Some say my "philosophy" is all that matters.

Others say that if my writings are any good at all, it is in spite of their bad philosophy.

Bearing all this in mind, I have switched to poetry.

As to illustrations of my novels. That decision was in the sagacious hands of the magazine publishers. I managed for the most part to keep the illustrations out of the novels when they appeared in book form, especially in regard to the later ones as I was able to have more say in the matter. Does anybody in his right mind want someone's drawing of Tess? Or Arabella Donn or Sue Bridehead? Phiz's caricatures for Dickens were fine: Mrs Gamp the drunken old nurse, Dora the child bride in David Copperfield*, even the sprite-like Little Dorrit. That was another time, forty or fifty years ago. Dickens had three or four illustrated books out before I was born. Illustrations (especially the satiric ones) were laudable in the old comic romances like those of Dickens — although of course there was no one* like *him. But illustrations have no place in studies such as mine, be they good or bad, into our modern aches and catastrophes.*

When I was much younger I thought the drawings by Helen
Paterson for my fourth novel, <u>Far from the Madding Crowd</u>, were
good, but I have come to oppose all book illustration for modern
novels. (Mention of that novel recalls to mind that when it first
appeared, anonymously, some critics – as above – thought it was by
George Eliot – a nice compliment, although even way back then I
wanted to be my own man.)

That much being said, I am in the process of bringing out a
collected edition of my Wessex Novels, and each novel shall have a
very "naturalistic" or realistic etching as a frontispiece. These
drawings will picture some geographical detail from the story, an
image that shall give – partly – the setting for the book: a country
road, a village main street, a pasture. No human figures will be
represented. It is my hope that the pictures will help set a mood.
If this be "illustrating" a novel, so be it. But I am steadfastly against
the very idea of novels of my sort being properly (or improperly)
"illustrated."

Yours truly
Thomas Hardy

Pretty good, eh?

Larry

PS   My gggf's letters to Mrs. Gaskell about the Bronte sisters were his
least successful tries. And from what I've learned at the New School,
I can put two and two together and figure out that he made the tactical
mistake of not asking her about her novels but mostly about her <u>Life of
Charlotte Bronte</u>. That book had caused Mrs. G a lot of trouble, and she
didn't want to discuss it. Although she had been very careful about
disguising names and keeping everything respectable, there was a
lawsuit from a Mrs. Robinson, claiming the book gave her a bad name.
This Mrs. Robinson had hired Charlotte Bronte's brother Branwell as a
live in tutor for her eleven year old kid. But then she had an affair with
young Branwell, and her husband kicked him out of the house. (The

name Mrs. Robinson from the movie "The Graduate" should ring a bell.) Mrs. Gaskell's biography was also attacked by the family of the clergyman who ran the Cowan Bridge School (Lowood in Jane Eyre) – the death house that killed two of Charlotte's sisters. In any case, Mrs. Gaskell was in no mood to answer my gggf's questions, especially the one about where in the world Charlotte Bronte had learned to make her woman characters like Jane Eyre and Lucy Snowe so passionate. We know today that Mrs. G in fact knew all about Charlotte's frustrated and absolutely fanatical love for her married professor over in Brussels in the 1840s – that was before she wrote her novels. His name was Constantin Heger, and he's the model for Paul Emmanuel in Villette and even to some extent for Rochester in Jane Eyre. But of course Mrs. Gaskell wouldn't let on to my gggf.

So on these Gaskell letters you can just wait till I send everything.

From: Nicholls@btinternet.com
To: L.Dickerson@verizon.net
29 September 2007

Larry

Fine on Mrs Gaskell. I'm waiting. The Hardy is perfectly splendid.

Stephen

Chapter Fourteen

From: L.Dickerson@verizon.net
To: Nicholls@btinternet.com
Oct. 2, 2007

Dear Stephen

As I am coming near the end, I'm wondering to myself about that word "Victorian." Gross handed out xeroxes of the first chapter of a book on Victorian sexuality by a Englishman named Michael Mason. Mason says that the Victorian Age – or even just the word Victorian – "awakens in us hostile feelings towards this particular past." The names of other eras don't do this. We don't feel "hostile" when we hear of the Age of Shakespeare, the 20th century, the Jazz Age, etc. The word Victorian "goes beyond the chronology" because even after Queen Victoria's death, the word was still applied not just to the period of when she was Queen, but to persons or beliefs we now think of as silly. And "the nub," says Mason, of this hostility is almost always Victorian attitudes towards sex. The word Victorian is often a "pejorative" – here meaning prudish or inhibited. I suppose it's like when someone says, "Oh, don't be so Victorian."

So far so good. But the main point of Mason's book – which, from this chapter, looks like pretty heavy going – is that the Victorians "didn't have any monopoly on sexual prohibitions." They inherited most of them, and there was "no abrupt change" when Queen Victoria took over.

Gross's point, on the other hand, is that it's really sad that the "baggage" of the word Victorian should sometimes "attach itself" to something as terrific as the Victorian Novel. Even for people who won't admit having any prejudice against the Victorians, the word still carries "negative overtones" – tones that you don't think you are hearing, but you are.

What do you think?

Yours
Larry

From: Nicholls@btinternet.com
To: L.Dickerson@verizon.net
4 October 2007

Dear Larry

The ideas you have mined from Michael Mason are to me quite thought provoking. I'd have to read the book to say anything worthwhile on the subject, and I am not prepared to do that. But I would hesitate to concur on his thesis of there being no abrupt change with Victoria's accession to the throne. Certainly there was an abrupt change at the top. In the forty or so years just prior to her becoming Queen in 1837, the royal family had been fantastically dissolute. "Mad King George III" (he did become insane) had seven profligate sons, including the heir apparent, the Prince Regent, later George IV. This George's only child, a young woman and heir to the throne, died early. The other possible progenitors of claimants to the throne, i.e., George IV's six brothers, had mistresses and plenty of illegitimate children, though none of these children could be heirs to the throne because they were bastards. The Duke of Kent, after the death of his oldest brother George's only child, did his "sad duty" and put aside his French mistress of ever so many years and married a young German princess who bore him a daughter. This child, Victoria, became the heir presumptive to the crown, and on the death of her uncle in 1837, when she was about eighteen, she became Queen of England. (English schoolboys have to know their royal lineage top to bottom.)

I recall that Lytton Strachey – usually thought of as the great debunker of all things Victorian – in his biography of Queen Victoria has a lovely passage on precisely the difference between her and her predecessors.

And Queen Victoria remained very "Victorian" all her life, a very long life as you well know. Till the end, for example, she not only abhorred the notion of divorce but held that a widowed woman should never remarry. She violently opposed women's rights. And I doubt she ever knew just what homosexual behaviour was. So I wonder about that part of Mason's thesis.

About the word <u>Victorian</u> and its implications and overtones, Mason seems indisputably on target. But let's hope that little of the stigma attached to the word obtains when combined in the phrase "the Victorian novel" – for many people the golden age of English prose fiction.

Best
Stephen

From: L.Dickerson@verizon.net
To: Nicholls@btinternet.com
Oct. 6, 2007

Stephen

   Very good. What exactly did this Lytton Strachey say? You could look it up.

Larry

From: Nicholls@btinternet.com
To: L.Dickerson@verizon.net
10 October 2007

Larry,

All right, I've just "looked it up." Strachey writes that when the new,
18-year-old Queen Victoria held her very first Council:

> What, above all, struck everybody with overwhelming force was
> the contrast between Queen Victoria and her uncles. The nasty
> old men, debauched and selfish, pig-headed and ridiculous, with
> their perpetual burden of debts, confusions, and disreputabilities
> – they had vanished like the snows of winter, and here at last,
> crowned and radiant, was the spring.

I remember being struck by these words years ago at university.

Best
Stephen

From: L.Dickerson@verizon.net
To: Nicholls@btinternet.com
Oct. 11, 2007

Dear Stephen

Well, there you are. Very nice, and it makes Mason look weak on the
"abrupt change" business. I'm starting to agree all the more with Gross
when he says that the safe position to have about popular beliefs – like
believing that the Victorians were all sexually repressed and religious
into the bargain – is that those beliefs are at best half true. So, you take
my Victorians on the sexual issue:

Dickens "put away" his wife of 20 years (and ten children) and had a mistress for 12 years.

George Eliot lived with a married man about 25 years – until he died.

Wilkie Collins believed that marriage degraded women, and he lived many years with a working class woman, and he had two children with another working class woman, sometimes going back and forth between the two houses.

Butler was a gay man with a slight heterosexual side to him that had him going weekly to the same prostitute for about 20 years – almost out of a sense of duty.

Thackeray and Trollope were pretty straight shooters. As far as we know. Thackeray's wife went crazy early on in their marriage and had to be put into an institution – so he had a madwoman in the attic, like Rochester in Jane Eyre. Charlotte Bronte didn't know this, but she admired Vanity Fair so much that she dedicated the second edition of Jane Eyre to Thackeray. This added fuel to the ridiculous rumor that "Jane Eyre," that is, Currer Bell – that is, Charlotte Bronte – had been a governess for Thackeray's daughters and then became his mistress. She was supposed to have turned him into Rochester, and he was supposed to have turned her into Becky Sharp. When a nosy American woman asked Thackeray if there had been such an affair, he told her, "Yes, Madame, and there were two children born to that unholy union and I slew them both with my own hand." Thackeray did have a sad platonic love affair with a good friend's wife. Trollope from age 45 on had a (platonic again) 20 year crush on a young American woman named Kate Field.

Charlotte Bronte, though not really on my list, behaved herself, except not really when you figure in her wild attachment for her married Professor Heger, as per my recent stuff on her.

Mrs. Gaskell behaved herself.

Then, on the religious issue, were these great Victorians pious Christians?

Dickens and Thackeray and Trollope were at best kind of "nominal" Christians. Thackeray had a real skeptical streak in him but didn't feel free to express it. I've read that Trollope regarded the Church of England – of which he was a member – as a branch of the Civil Service, like the Post Office.

I'd give you Charlotte Bronte. As for her sister Emily, to me Wuthering Heights reads like a book by a pagan.

Mrs. Gaskell being a Unitarian was a kind of half-Christian.

George Eliot (and Mr. George Eliot), Butler, and Hardy were nonbelievers. Not to mention Darwin.

So much for the common belief that the Victorians were all sexually hung up and religious. But at the same time I think it is true that many people are still bothered or annoyed – even "unconsciously" – at the word "Victorian" even in the phrase "the Victorian novel."

Yours
Larry

From: Nicholls@btinternet.com
To: L.Dickerson@verizon.net
12 October 2007

Larry

I dare say you are becoming a regular authority in these matters. Nicely done.

Stephen

From: L.Dickerson@verizon
To: Nicholls@btinternet.com
Oct. 13, 2007

Stephen

Hell, it's no big deal. I'm just filling in my education, you might say.
I'm mopping up small little things now – a couple of difficult words
still to decipher, checking out some remaining annotations, etc. And
then for a quick run through the whole thing. I'll be done in less than a
month. Say three weeks. You could say I'm as good as done.

Larry

From: Nicholls@btinternet.com
To: L.Dickerson@verizon.net
17 October 2007

Dear Larry

It's good that you are at what you call the mopping-up stage because
there is a bit of an upheaval, or better stated a slight changing of the
guard, at Christie's. Your humble servant is to be "moved upstairs" to a
kind of vice presidency. My new title is a tad inflated as there are any
number of vice presidents in an operation as large as this. But even
after the change happens, I shall try to keep myself involved with your
(I almost said our) project and will tell my replacement to give you and
your work careful attention.

Best
Stephen

From: L.Dickerson@verizon.net
To: Nicholls@btinternet.com
Oct. 18, 2007

Dear Stephen

I take it you meant to break the news gently. Just tell me who the
hell I'll be dealing with. Christ almighty, I do hope you can keep your

hand in this particular pie because I've grown attached to working with you.

Yours
Larry

I <u>am</u> just about at the end, but I wish to god you were around for the final push.

◡◞

From: Nicholls@btinternet.com
To: L.Dickerson@verizon.net
19 October 2007

Dear Larry

I too have grown attached to our working together. But, in fact, my promotion will have happened as of the day after tomorrow. I have explained your project in very considerable detail to my most capable successor. I've even taken the liberty of copying out those of your emails that contained transcribed letters. Address

CharlieDover@christies.co.uk

Yours affectionately
Stephen

We can of course occasionally "shoot the breeze" on other matters privately, but send all official business to Charlie.

◡◞

From: L.Dickerson@verizon.net
To: CharlieDover@christies.co.uk
Oct. 20, 2007

Dear Charlie Dover

   Stephen Nicholls gave me your name and said he explained my
project to you in detail. I'll be reporting to you on my progress, my
transcriptions, etc.

                                        Yours truly
                                        Larry Dickerson

From: CharlieDover@christies.co.uk
To: L.Dickerson@verizon.net
22 October 2007

Dear Larry Dickerson

Yes, I have moved into Stephen's office, and It's also a big change for
me. This is naturally a busy time, but at Stephen's direction, I have your
entire file printed out in hard copy before me now, and I must say your
project sounds fascinating and important. I understand the drill, how
you wish to make the first transcriptions yourself, provide annotation,
commentary, etc. Any assistance I can offer you, just say the word. I look
forward to working with you.

We can keep Stephen in the picture, occasionally, even though he'll be
frightfully busy.

Yours
Charlie Dover

From: L.Dickerson@verizon.net
To: CharlieDover@christies.co.uk
Oct. 22, 2007

Dear Charlie Dover

　　Thanks. This will be my shortest email. I'm usually too talkative.

                              Yours truly
                              Larry Dickerson

⌒

From: L.Dickerson@verizon.net
To: Nicholls@btinternet.com
Oct. 22, 2007

Dear Stephen

　　Don't mean to bother you, just sending a line to say I've heard from Charlie Dover and he sounds like a decent guy although one short email is not much to go on. I'll take your word for it that he knows what he is doing.
　　Don't mean to interrupt your million dollar doings in your new position.

                              Yours
                              Larry

⌒

From: Nicholls@btinternet.com
To: L.Dickerson@verizon.net
23 October 2007

She. Not he. Charlie stands for Charlotte.

From: L.Dickerson@verizon.net
To: Nicholls@btinternet.com
Oct. 24, 2007

    Christ in heaven why didn't you say so? I might have made an ass of myself and said something off color. God knows I'm careful enough with you just because you are an English man – but an English <u>woman</u>! God knows how long this might have gone on if I hadn't emailed you. "Charlie" – what the hell kind of a name is that for a girl?

From: Nicholls@btinternet.com
To: L.Dickerson@verizon.net
25 October 2007

Larry

Calm down, old fellow. Charlie is very good at what she does, which is what you want. What difference does it make? She's talented, capable, industrious, knowledgeable, and friendly. And attractive into the bargain.

As to the name, I think if it were male it would be Charley.

Charlie is a common nickname here for Charlotte.

Stephen

From: L.Dickerson@verizon.net
To: Nicholls@btinternet.com
Oct. 25, 2007

Stephen

Charley Smarley. And you ask what difference does it make? Plenty. You should know that. Like, no more saying I don't care a rat's ass for something. I'll have to be always watching my myself as to what I say, and it's damn annoying. But more than that, I was doing so well with you, coming along, learning the trade – as they say – picking up things from you but also having a feeling that you were enjoying the give and take with me. Now that's all gone. It's worse than getting a new doctor after 35 years. He hands off your records and disappears.

Larry

From: Nicholls@btinternet.com
To: L.Dickerson@verizon.net
26 October 2007

Dear Larry

All right, it is a change, but not the breaking off of a 35-year connection. Besides, as I've said, we can still keep in touch "informally." As for Charlie, you be straightforward and forthcoming with her, and she'll be the same with you. She's a wonderful woman. I should say wonderful person.

Best
Stephen

From: L.Dickerson@verizon.net
To: Nicholls@btinternet.com
Oct. 26, 2007

Christ, it sounds like you're in love with her.

From: Nicholls@btinternet.com
To: L.Dickerson@verizon.net
27 October 2007

In England we say "keen on" a person.

From: L.Dickerson@verizon.net
To: Nicholls@btinternet.com
Oct. 28, 2007

Well, are you "keen" on her?

From: Nicholls@btinternet.com
To: L.Dickerson@verizon.net
29 October 2007

I'm a married man.

From: L.Dickerson@verizon.net
To: Nicholls@btinternet.com
Oct. 29, 2007

I didn't ask if you were married, I asked if you are keen on her.

⌒

From: Nicholls@btinternet.com
To: L.Dickerson@verizon.net
30 October 2007

Dear Larry

Let's pursue this particular subject no further. You are in her hands, "so to speak," and I wish you well.

Stephen

⌒

From: L.Dickerson@verizon.net
To: Nicholls@btinternet.com
Nov. 1, 2007

Dear Stephen

   Well, I wish you well, too. I remember Gross, who was forever mentioning the <u>The New Yorker</u>, telling us that the boss there was once so angry with an employee who quit him for a job in Los Angeles that he closed his letter to the guy with "Well, God bless you, God damn it."

Larry

⌒

From: Nicholls@btinternet.com
To: L.Dickerson@verizon.net
2 November 2007

Larry

At least you yourself haven't lost your sceptical grip and said to me
"God bless you in your new job," and for that we should both be
grateful.

Still, as far as your project goes, since it is nearing completion and as
you are about to return officially to Christie's, I am really "out of the
loop" as you say in America.

Stephen

⌒

From: L.Dickerson@verizon.net
To: Nicholls@btinternet.com
Nov. 2, 2007

Dear Stephen

Okay, okay. But I don't use "out of the loop." That's what our half ass
presidents and politicians say when they don't want to be involved in
big mistakes like Iran Contra or the war in Iraq. I bet your Tony Blair
might say he was out of the loop when he tailed along with G W Bush.
Oops, I never like to even mention his name. This change at Christie's
has me rattled. Why did Blair make such an ass of himself?

Larry

⌒

From: Nicholls@btinternet.com
To: L.Dickerson@verizon.net
3 November 2007

Dear Larry

To use an American expression, you've got me there. In England everyone argues about why Blair did it – i.e., go to war and the rest of it. No one has a convincing answer. As the cliché says, it's a puzzle wrapped in an enigma. Maybe his religiosity, together with a conviction that your President Bush and America were top dog, made him want to be part of the undertaking. The whole situation is depressing.

Stephen

From: L.Dickerson@verizon.net
To: Nicholls@btinternet.com
Nov. 4, 2007

Dear Stephen

It's a hell of a lot <u>more</u> depressing for an American. We have about 150 thousand troops in Iraq, you have 5 thousand and the Poles and Italians have six men each. Coalition forces. What horseshit. I don't talk about it. For one thing, here in New York City our president – I can't bring myself to mention his name – if he were running for any office would get about nine votes, total. But then most of the rest of the U.S. hates New York. They look on us – in no particular order – as a bunch of blacks, Puerto Ricans, illegals, gays, union people, rich "limousine liberals," and especially Jews, liberal Jews.

Let's get back to Victorian days. Gross told us that a famous historian named something Young said, "If a man could choose one decade to be young in – and his name was Young – it would be the 1850s."

Larry

From: Nicholls@btinternet.com
To: L.Dickerson@verizon.net
5 November 2007

Dear Larry

It's a thought. Why not pass it on to Charlie, your new Christie's email correspondent. The historian was G. M. Young.

Best
Stephen

From: L.Dickerson@verizon.net
To: Nicholls@btinternet.com
Nov. 6, 2007

Dear Stephen

Righto. This will be my last email to you for a while. Send me news privately, like when you break the world record selling Cezannes and Impressionists for millions. Okay, it's back to nickel and dime stuff for me and Charlie.

And of course I'd have to change G.M. Young's "young man" to "young person" – fircrissakes.

Larry

Chapter Sixteen

From: CharlieDover@christies.co.uk
To: L.Dickerson@verizon.net
9 November 2007

Dear Larry (if I may)

Here I am only scarcely two weeks into my new job, and they are
sending me to Christie's New York – four days next week. We are
auctioning Impressionist pen and ink drawings, and I was involved in
organizing the exhibition.

Shall we meet up? How about supper Wednesday 14th?

And I'll be Charlie.

From: L.Dickerson@verizon.net
To: CharlieDover@christies.co.uk
Nov. 9, 2007

Dear Charlie

   Great that you're coming to New York. How about a restaurant
called Il Cantinori at 32 East 10th Street at 7 pm? Wednesday 14th.

Yours
Larry

From: CharlieDover@christies.co.uk
To: L.Dickerson@verizon.net
9 November 2007

You're on. Don't forget to bring a sampling of your letters with you.

Charlie

From: L.Dickerson@verizon.net
To: CharlieDover@christies.co.uk
Nov. 9, 2007

Dear Charlie

　　Okay. It'll be my coming out party as far as these manuscript letters are concerned. Just don't let me spill any water, or worse, on them.

　　　　　　　　　　　　　　Yours
　　　　　　　　　　　　　　Larry

From: CharlieDover@christies.co.uk
To: L.Dickerson@verizon.net
9 November 2007

Dear Larry

Don't bring the originals to a restaurant! Bring your photocopies.

Charlie

From: L.Dickerson@verizon.net
To: CharlieDover@christies.co.uk
Nov. 9, 2007

Dear Charlie

I'm working from the originals. I thought you knew that. But I guess I'd better get those copies made.

Yours
Larry

From: CharlieDover@christies.co.uk
To: L.Dickerson@verizon.net
9 November 2007

Dear Larry

I know I'm new on your case and that you had a private arrangement with Stephen. And while I knew you didn't want anyone seeing the originals until you had transcribed everything, I had no idea that you were still working from the originals. Don't. That's my simple advice. You shouldn't be handling precious letters. In some rare book rooms they make you put on white cotton gloves before you can handle a manuscript. Additionally, if you have photocopies, you can mark them up, circle words that are troubling you, etc. Sometimes holding a page up to the light at different angles helps in deciphering difficult words. You can also take a photocopy of a sentence or two that contains the troubling word and show it to a friend. Sometimes a word difficult for one person just leaps out at a new pair of eyes.

Forgive my being so bullying on this matter of working from photocopies. But in this I know I'm right. Till Wednesday.

Yours
Charlie

⌒

From: L.Dickerson@verizon.net
To: CharlieDover@christies.co.uk
Nov. 9, 2007

Dear Charlie

My God you're making me nervous about these originals. Actually, Stephen once told me I should have them insured but I pooh poohed the idea. I understand this kind of "art" insurance is pretty steep. Well that's water over the dam. Maybe I <u>should</u> have been nervous all along. What you say makes me feel I ought to be glad to get rid of them – for a price, of course. What If I had a fire or something? I should probably have been keeping them in a strongbox and keeping the strongbox in the refrigerator. Well, too late. I've got practically everything done. Will xerox all my originals tomorrow and on Wednesday I will bring xeroxes of, I suppose, Dickens – he's my biggest fish, right?

I'm looking forward to meeting you.

Yours
Larry

⌒

From: CharlieDover@btinternet.com
To: Nicholls@btinternet.com
14 November 2007

Dear Stephen

By separate Christie's email I have sent you a report on the Impressionist drawings. It all looks terrific and will be a great show.

I've just had a fascinating dinner with your friend Dickerson. I'll report on him tomorrow – right now I'm too tired (dinner was three hours).

Hugs
Charlie

I've invited him up to the New York showroom tomorrow for the tail end of the morning sale of American manuscripts.

⌒

From: CharlieDover@btinternet.com
To: Nicholls@btinternet.com
15 November 2007

Dear Stephen

All right, here's my private email report on your pen pal Larry Dickerson. But first I will announce that early next week he will post us photocopies of all the original materials; following that, in a couple of weeks, he will send his transcriptions and notes in case we wish to incorporate some of his work into the catalogue; and, finally, at about that same time, he'll send the originals.

I've certainly gotten to know your American. I realize you are fascinated by him, and I'm going to give you a full account because I'm all packed for the flight home tomorrow morning and have nothing, really, to do tonight. He would have gone out for supper yet again tonight, but as I had already seen him two days running, I told him I was working tonight and had to catch a plane in the morning, etc. I think he has a little crush on me. So I'm here in my room talking to you on this marvelous laptop computer.

I'll begin with last night's dinner. For starters, so to speak, he is younger looking than you'd expect from a retired bank worker of sixty-five. I expect he would strike most people as in his fifties. I think too that he, seven years a widower, was in a clumsy way thrilled to be out, at night, with a woman, and a woman considerably younger than himself. The restaurant was a most romantic (and expensive) place, and he gallantly tried at the end to pay or at the very least split the bill, but of course I put it on Christie's tab. I think he was altogether tickled pink with himself. What could I do but be kind and play along – though not very far of course. He's even thinking of coming to London to see me (and you) and to visit some of the places mentioned in his letters. He would love to see the Garrick Club, but I told him you have to be with a member. In which case he'll settle for the Dickens House on Doughty Street, or Onslow Square, where Thackeray lived. I told him about London blue plaques, and after dinner he insisted on showing me a couple of plaques, not blue of course, but right there on the street where the Italian restaurant is, 10th Street. (I'm not sure where East 10th and West 10th Streets part, but somewhere in the middle.) Mark Twain's house has a plaque, in which house, Dickerson explained, some dozen years ago a man high on drugs murdered his little six-year-old daughter – a famous case in New York City. A few doors away was the building where Emma Lazarus (the Statue of Liberty poet) lived, and the plaque even quotes the line, "Give me your tired, your poor, your huddled masses yearning to breathe free." Dickerson then pointed out an apartment, now a dentist's office, and bearing no plaque of any kind, at 44 West 10th Street, where William Faulkner once lived, though it was "ages ago" and ever so briefly. Dickerson knows the "super," i.e., superintendent, in the building, and when the super learned from Dickerson about his "literary work" – Dickerson talks about his interest in Victorian novelists with anybody who will listen to him – the super told Dickerson about Faulkner having lived there. Dickerson says proudly, "Nobody else knows about it." He has never read any Faulkner, he explains, because all his time is taken up with "his" novelists.

Dickerson and I parted with a peck on the cheek. I could see he was enthusiastic. But his interest in Victorian writers is absolutely genuine and more than merely enthusiastic. It's well informed. I suspect he is anxious for us to see how good a job he has done transcribing and annotating the letters. As you may know, I talked – scared him really – into photocopying everything. He brought along a handful of Dickens photocopies; he also brought his relevant transcriptions with him, and they looked very accurate. And I expect he will have done a good job throughout. He's really intelligent but affects a kind of low-brow American blockheadedness. In fact, there were times when I could see that he was really bright and knowledgeable – more so than his long trail of correspondence with you would have us believe. For example, we got onto the subject of the Impressionists – I told him briefly what I was doing at Christie's New York – and he asked very sensible questions. And then, just as quickly, he lapsed back into reaction, saying he likes nothing that came after the Impressionists, or certainly nothing later than Cézanne – whom he seems enamoured of. He's "awed" that I should be working with Cézanne drawings. Dickerson says he likes paintings with "pictures on them." "You don't really know," he says, "if these abstract painters can even draw." He has two old Piranesi prints (Vedute di Roma) that he hoped were worth some money. But at the bank he met an Italian (a "real Italian," not "an American with a name ending in a vowel who thinks Frank Sinatra the greatest figure in all music"), and this Italian fellow deflated him by saying that the Vedute di Roma are so common in Italy that every dentist has one on the wall of his waiting room. In any event Dickerson plans to take his two prints out of the frames and see what an auction house thinks. I told him to try Swann's because we at Christie's would handle Piranesi only in the complete set, very early state, and perfect condition. Further deflation.

You may quite rightly ask how I know so much about him. Well, you know from all those emails how loquacious he is. But, funnily enough –

during the interstices, so to say – he listens intently and carefully takes in whatever you are saying. If at any point you lose him, he doesn't fake it; he interjects, "Who's that?" When I told him, for example, of our handling some Blake drawings lately, he interrupted, "Who's that?" And he is preternaturally interested in the prices things bring at auction. This is, I suppose, understandable as he may well be sitting on a fortune. When I mentioned our recent sale of some E M Forster letters, after first asking who EMF was, he immediately wanted to know how much the letters fetched at auction. But then he followed up by inquiring which book of Forster's was his best known. When I told him Passage to India, he said that, come to think of it, he may have heard of that book because his wife had "dragged" him to see the movie years ago. But he's anxious to read almost any English novel recommended by "someone who knows what he's talking about," and so when he has the time he plans to "look into" Passage to India. "Look into" is a favourite phrase of his. He tells a story about Chicago's old Mayor Daley – the father of the present mayor – and Saul Bellow. The story goes (and Dickerson is a good storyteller) that forty or fifty years ago Mayor Daley père had to present Bellow with an award as Chicago's Man of the Year for writing Herzog. Reporters, always after Daley, ask him "if he had read Mr. Bellow's book?" and Daley replies, "I've looked into it "

I kept telling myself I was doing this as a service to you, who are so curious about the chap you've been corresponding with for so long. On the other hand, I found myself fascinated. He is, as they say, a study. So American in his enthusiasm, innocence, willingness to learn; and a bit in awe, by now, of all things English. Still, he is trying hard not to be what he himself calls a "serial bore." When he had been going on too long about his interests in Victorian writers, he caught himself, said so, and plied me with questions. At first I thought he was going to say, "Let's see, what are your hobbies?" But no; he wanted to know how I got interested in working at a place like Christie's; whether dealing with such material had increased or decreased my interest in rare objects: "A person who is crazy about, let's say Cézanne, must be excited out of his mind to hold an actual Cézanne in his hands – right?" But then doesn't it become "old hat" if you do it all the time? For a moment I thought he was going to reach for the example of married people having sex. But no. He was discreet almost to the point of puritanical.

He wanted to know what I had "majored in in college." At the mention of Cambridge I could see his jaw drop. Class conscious in regard to universities as we Brits are, Americans, if he's any indication, are even more so. Cambridge is "like Harvard or Princeton or Yale." He asked me where you had been to college, and when I told him Oxford, he again said this was "like the Ivy League." He pronounces the words "Ivy League" with a combination of awe and annoyance. He himself dropped out of "a third-rate place" in New Jersey and could not have even <u>thought</u> of going to one of these schools, but if he did, it would have been Princeton because it is in New Jersey. He seemed always on edge about New Jersey, anxious to defend it, though I was in no way inclined to denigrate it and wouldn't have known why I should have. He explained that New Jersey has a bad reputation – he didn't say exactly why – and that some comedians get a laugh just by saying out loud the words "New Jersey" or calling it "the Garden State." He is in fact a "transplant" to New York City, but he still has a warm spot for New Jersey. And he also explained that New Jersey is the most crowded of all fifty states – "the most people per square mile" – which is "no big deal," <u>but</u> he read somewhere a few years ago that New Jersey had the highest or second highest per capita income of all fifty states. This in spite of poor cities with slums, like Newark and Camden. (Are <u>all</u> American place names English? Clearly not – but most seem to be.)

A confession: his being such a naive and outspoken man, I thought I ought in passing to allude to the fact that I am Jewish, lest he – and this was really unfair to him and unworthy of me – slip in some little even unintended anti-Semitism in his loose-style speech. But not a bit of it. He was amazed that there were English Jews: "I thought all Englishmen were WASPs," he says. But as for Jews, since coming from New Jersey twenty years ago he finds that all his new friends are Jewish. Not the old cliché about "some of my best friends" – but <u>all</u> of them. A fine religion, he says. Nowhere near as silly as Catholicism, for example, in which faith a lot of his old friends in New Jersey were brought up. What he likes about the Jewish religion is that "you don't have to believe very much," or, come to that, you can be a Jew and "disbelieve in God." Then he forced on me a "Jewish joke" – heard from a Jew – about a man trying to sell his friend an elephant for $800. The friend says, "Don't be ridiculous. What the hell would I want an elephant for?" The first man keeps lowering his price, $700, $600; and the other keeps saying, "You're crazy. What would I do with an elephant?" Finally the first says, "All right, for you, something special. Two elephants, $500." To which the other responds, "Now you're talking."

Enough or more than enough about last night's dinner. I'm talking too much. Must have caught the bug from Dickerson.

As for today's meeting up at Christie's Rockefeller Plaza, I'll be brief. The news is not altogether good. The place, as you know, is really quite spectacular. Larry was "blown away"; and he goes so far as to say that the LeWitt mural in the lobby "almost makes me change my mind about abstract art." As we had arranged, he arrived for the tail end of the morning session of American manuscripts; he watched every move intently, took it all in, and asked good questions. The time came to 12:30, and he wanted to show me photocopies he brought with him of the letters with the Thackeray drawings on them, and so we went to the nearest place for lunch. And while we were poring over the Thackeray letters (the drawings are small but charming, and so very "Thackerayan"), who should stop by our table but Phillip Osgood. He told us he had manuscripts coming up for auction in the afternoon session, and he had just attended the morning session. Osgood knows me slightly and says he knows you from his visits to Christie's London. I'm not sure, but it's just possible he followed us out of the salesroom. That part may be paranoia on my part. In any case I was not delighted, as you can imagine, to have this high-end, Upper East Side manuscripts dealer descend upon us. Of course I introduced Dickerson. And since Dickerson and I were looking so animatedly at his photocopies, I could hardly help but tell him (briefly and guardedly) what we were doing. Then Osgood gives his card to Dickerson, saying, genially, that he is in the manuscript game himself and that if Dickerson ever finds another batch of important letters, he should consider consulting him. Dickerson takes the card and says cheerfully that "of course" he doesn't have a card but that if he ever inherits another box of letters, he'll try running them by him. Osgood makes a little joke about not having exactly caught Dickerson's name – "It's not 'Dickens' surely?" Once that is cleared up, he disappears as quickly as he appeared.

Miss you,
Hugs
Charlie

From: L.Dickerson@verizon.net
To: CharlieDover@christies.co.uk
Nov. 19, 2007

Dear Charlie

Thanks for the great meal – and lunch too – and most especially for the tour of Christie's Rockefeller Plaza. I can't believe I'm involved with an outfit like Christie's. Is Christie's King Street like that? So nice to meet you and gab away about everything. I hope we can meet and talk again sometime soon.

But, okay! Will wonders never cease? By international air mail I sent you today xeroxes of all the originals – 109 letters from the big shots and a few more than that from my gggf, about 230 letters in all, some taking up two or three pages each. And I had a hell of a wait at the Post Office. They seem to think they can stop terrorism by asking you if you have a bomb in your package. What do they expect the bomber to say? "Yes, here, please take my bomb"?

Let me know that the photocopies arrive.

Now that I've sent these off, forgive me while I send you my opinionated take on the whole business so far. I have by now read most of the books mentioned in my letters. And unlike some of my gggf's correspondents, I have no hesitation in saying what novels I liked and what I didn't like. I like <u>Vanity Fair</u> and Trollope best. I don't like <u>Wuthering Heights</u> – it's a teenage girl's book in my humble opinion.

And I hate <u>Villette</u> — too depressing. <u>Jane Eyre</u> is an improvement on <u>Wuthering Heights</u> and <u>Villette</u>. <u>The Mill on the Floss</u> is great in places, but I don't like the ending, and neither does anybody else from what I have read. George Eliot had backed herself into a corner. <u>The Woman in White</u>, as I told Stephen, is engrossing, but it's a bit too much in its twists and turns of plot. And — though how should I really know except by what some expert tells me? — I think it's poorly written. Hardy's <u>Tess of the D'Urbervilles</u> wiped me out, in spite of his big words and abstract nouns. It's a fantastic "read." The mystery is how can anything that sad make you feel good. Butler's <u>Erewhon</u> is good in stretches, not so great in others. The "Musical Banks" chapter is worth the price of admission, as we say. I never got around to Mrs. Gaskell. Dickens is a problem. The first third of <u>David Copperfield</u> is tops. As one Dickens biographer says, it's the most "radiant" account of childhood ever written, and really a separate novel in itself. No there's nothing like the first part of <u>David Copperfield</u>. But the last two thirds of the book — except for the "blessed lunatic" Mr. Dick, and some of the Mr. Micawber's funny talk, is a bore, and the ending is sentimental "claptrap," whatever exactly claptrap is. <u>Great Expectations</u> — which everyone but Dickens seems to think is his best novel — is like <u>David Copperfield</u>, better in the beginning than in the end. And then there's that terrific Podsnap stuff in <u>Our Mutual Friend</u>. So Dickens is a bag of gold with some manure mixed in. Maybe there's less gold in Thackeray as a whole, but he's gold or at least silver on every page of <u>Vanity Fair</u>. As for childhood, Maggie in <u>The Mill on the Floss</u> is also terrific. I know people in this game are forever quoting Virginia Woolf as to saying that George Eliot's <u>Middlemarch</u> is one of the handful of novels in English written for grown ups. I don't believe it, and the only mention of it in the correspondence is Samuel Butler saying he hated it.

There you have my picks. I know that many people say it's wrong to "rank" novelists, but I don't see that. Say what you think is what I believe.

Yours
Larry

Copy this to my busy friend Stephen the vice president.

From: CharlieDover@christies.co.uk
To: L.Dickerson@verizon.net
19 November 2007

Dear Larry

I too very much enjoyed our time together. I doubt I'll be getting to New York again for a considerable while. You must come to London. King Street headquarters is not as grand as the Rockefeller Plaza building, but it's impressive in its own old-fashioned way. You must visit us.

The photocopies arrived in fine order, and we shall get to evaluating them and assigning high and low estimates for the nine lots and an approximate total for the aggregate, again with a high and low estimate.

As for your literary judgements, they seem to me to be very well informed. And yes, why not offer one's likes and dislikes? No disputing tastes, right? My own tastes in these novelists differ from yours, of course. I shouldn't say "of course," but you know what I mean. Different people like different things. I've never been a big Trollope fan, but then I have read relatively little Trollope. I think I had to read <u>The Way We Live Now</u> at Cambridge. I've never read Butler, so don't have an opinion. Dickens was so much a part of my schooling, from the beginning through university, that I hate him and love him according to whether I had to read him or did so on my own. As for <u>Vanity Fair</u>, I am willing to take your word for it. I was too young when I had to read it. I gather it is a book for grown-ups. When I was studying for A levels — tests to get into university — I was mad about Hardy, especially <u>Tess</u>. I loved <u>Wuthering Heights</u>, and nothing you can say about it being a young girl's book would change my mind — unless I were to read it again and find you are right. But I don't want to do that. Ditto for <u>Jane Eyre</u>. <u>Villette</u>, as I remember, is powerful stuff, but as you say, depressing. Still, I put it very high. As for Mrs Gaskell, I suggest that when you have time you "look into" a little book of hers called <u>Cranford</u> — or even better yet, <u>Wives</u>

and Daughters, a somewhat Trollopian novel. On Wilkie Collins I agree with you. That leaves my favourite, George Eliot. For me she's very special. Adam Bede and Mill on the Floss are in my view truly great novels. And as for Middlemarch, I don't for a moment care what your man Samuel Butler thought of it. Virginia Woolf may indeed have overstated the case, but not by a whole lot. When I was going off to university, like many other young women in my position, I secretly saw myself as a sort of enlightened Dorothea Brooke. (Most of us had read the book.) But thank God I never married a Casaubon.

Back to work for me.

Yours
Charlie

From: L.Dickerson@verizon.net
To: CharlieDover@christies.co.uk
Nov. 20, 2007

Dear Charlie

    I don't get the Dorothea Brooke and Casaubon stuff – since I never read Middlemarch, that novel for grown ups.

                                        Larry

From: CharlieDover@christies.co.uk
To: L.Dickerson@verizon.net
20 November 2007

Dear Larry

Dorothea is an idealistic, enthusiastic, innocent young woman intent on doing something worthwhile. She foolishly thinks she can be of service (to the world of thought, I suppose) by marrying a dried-up stick of an old man, a pedant named Casaubon, who is intent on discovering "the key to all mythologies" – an intellectual goose chase. The marriage is a complete disaster, though luckily Casaubon dies fairly soon. Myself, I've come close to marrying a couple of times but in any event have not made a mistake like hers. Maybe I'll never settle down and marry.

Yours
Charlie

⟨⟶

From: L.Dickerson@verizon.net
To: CharlieDover@christies.co.uk
Nov. 20, 2007

Dear Charlie

    Don't be ridiculous. Like George Eliot herself, you'll find Mr. Right someday soon. And I'll read Middlemarch and keep an eye on Dorothea Brooke.

                                                    Larry

⟨⟶

From: CharlieDover@christies.co.uk
To: L.Dickerson@verizon.net
21 November 2007

Larry

The novel, and Dorothea's story, come to a somewhat muted ending.

Charlie

From: L.Dickerson@verizon.net
To: CharlieDover@christies.co.uk
Nov. 21, 2007

Dear Charlie

   Christ, we all come to muted endings. My money is totally on you doing fine!

                                                        Larry

From: CharlieDover@christies.co.uk
To: L.Dickerson@verizon.net
12 November 2007

Thanks.

Chapter Seventeen

Phillip Osgood
Autographs & Manuscripts
757 Madison Avenue
New York, NY 10021

Mr. Larry Dickerson
27 East 13th Street
New York, NY 10003

November 22, 2007

Dear Mr. Dickerson,

I am pleased to have met you at lunch the other day. Please forgive me
the liberty I am taking by writing and asking you if you have had a
second opinion as to the value of your manuscript materials. There can
be no harm in asking a second opinion in such matters. People do it all
the time. How many letters from Victorian novelists do you have?

Yours truly
Phillip Osgood

From: L.Dickerson@verizon.net
To: phil@osgoodms.com
Nov. 24, 2007

Dear Mr. Osgood,

Thanks for your letter. How did you get my address? Not that I mind.
I'm getting your email off your card. I myself, naturally, don't have cards.

I have 109 "famous" letters (Dickens, Thackeray, Trollope, George Eliot,
Hardy, Wilkie Collins, Samuel Butler, et al) and 120 letters (copies) from my
great-great-grandfather to them. I've never thought about a second
opinion. I know Christie's is big time, and I figured I couldn't do any better
anywhere. Besides, I feel bound to Christie's, especially Stephen
Nicholls. I've been exchanging emails with him for about a year, and
now also for some time with Charlie Dover, a very nice young woman.

Yours
Larry Dickerson

From: phil@osgoodms.com
To: L.Dickerson@verizon.net
November 24, 2007

Dear Mr. Dickerson,

I found your regular mail address the old-fashioned way – from the
phone book. You're the only Lawrence Dickerson in the Manhattan
phone book. But I will now switch to email. By way of further
introducing myself, I sent a recent illustrated catalog of my offerings,
some of which coincide nicely with your own interests.

I understand the situation exactly and can readily see why you would
hesitate to have another party give an estimate on the value of your

materials. Still, there's presumably a lot at stake here. Think of how we are all encouraged to get second opinions in matters of health, operations, etc. What is there to lose? Has Christie's given you a contract?

Yours truly
Phillip Osgood

From: L.Dickerson@verizon.net
To: phil@osgoodms.com
Nov. 25, 2007

Dear Mr. Osgood,

Christie's hasn't sent me an estimate or a contract yet. They are working on their estimate, or I should say estimates, because the plan is to divide up the collection by separate authors – nine of them. I have just recently sent Christie's photocopies of all the originals. It took me a year to get the letters to them because I wanted to make my own transcriptions first, and Christie's has been very patient with me. My idea is to self publish both sides of the correspondence as a book, after the auction. I am told by one of these publish-yourself companies that they can do the whole thing for me in about a month.

I'd have to think it over a lot, the idea of me getting a second opinion.

Yours
Larry Dickerson

Your Catalog bowls me over. You are in a different league than me. I don't live in a world where people pay thousands of dollars for a scribbled note from Thomas Jefferson – or a long letter from Darwin for which you're asking $6000. My God, where do people get money to pay like that?

From: phil@osgoodms.com
To: L.Dickerson@verizon.net
November 25, 2007

Dear Mr. Dickerson,

As I said previously, I can understand your hesitation. But look at it as a completely nonbinding look-see you would be giving me. And by the bye, it is in any case as good as certain that I would be one of the bidders on your materials at the Christie's auction. Sleep on my offer of a second evaluation.

Now to another matter. And here I can afford to be blunt. You must not look on your work of transcriptions and annotations as a candidate for self-publishing. For such a trove as yours I could line up a genuine publisher tomorrow. A "real" publisher would not knock it off in a month like those silly self-publishing outfits, but would carefully edit all your transcriptions, check out your annotations, etc. This may take a year, but to have a legitimate book from a legitimate publisher would be well worth the delay: there's self-esteem for you as editor; there's as good as a guarantee that the book will be widely reviewed; and there would also be royalties, though admittedly not huge for a scholarly production such as this. Nonetheless, many college and university libraries, students of the Victorian novel, and so-called "literary" readers would feel obliged to own a book such as this. I urge you to consult further with me. Moreover, you must provide an introduction, no matter how short, explaining how you came to possess your collection.

Yours truly
Phillip Osgood

PS As for my catalog, you must realize that you are in this world, like it or not. Your letters are, I can tell even before seeing them, in the "league" that I deal with. Your authors are big-time players. As to why people with money spend it as they do, your guess is as good as mine; but you should bear in mind that collecting is a kind of "gentle madness," as someone once put it very nicely.

⌒⌐

From: L.Dickerson@verizon.net
To: phil@osgoodms.com
Nov. 25, 2007

Dear Mr. Osgood,

Thanks so much for your advice on publishing. I'll certainly consult with you before I commit myself anywhere. And I'll write out a little one page introduction about my great-great-grandfather and how the letters descended to me.

I've been thinking about that second opinion business. I might send you a set of the xeroxes, provided they are strictly for your eyes, with you telling no one about them and promising me a quick return of the xeroxes.

Yours
Larry Dickerson

I still feel that a retired personal banker like myself doesn't really belong in the world you talk about. On the other hand, I guess I've been lucky to be pushed into it, as they say. I suppose both me, a seller, and you, a buyer and a seller both, should be grateful for the crazy people who pay such prices. Not that I've sold anything yet.

⌒⌐

From: phil@osgoodms.com
To: L.Dickerson@verizon.net
November 25, 2007

Dear Mr. Dickerson,

It goes without saying that I would agree to your conditions for giving me a look at your materials.

Yours truly
Phillip Osgood

PS You're exactly right about being grateful for people who buy. Without buyers – well, nothing is worth anything.

⌣⟶

From: L.Dickerson@verizon.net
To: phil@osgoodms.com
Nov. 26, 2007

Dear Mr. Osgood,

   I'm mailing the photocopies to you today. I'm gearing up for another long wait standing on line at the Post Office.
   But my real problem is that I feel guilty as hell about sending these to another party other than Christie's. It seems like I'm being a traitor. I am going to tell Charlie Dover and Stephen Nicholls about me sending copies to you.

Yours
Larry Dickerson

⌣⟶

From: phil@osgoodms.com
To: L.Dickerson@verizon.net
November 30, 2007

Dear Mr. Dickerson,

The photocopies have arrived. Thank you. I understand your felt need
of telling Christie's, but in fact people get additional estimates all the
time. In any event, please wait a few days to see what I have to say.

Yours truly
Phillip Osgood

From: phil@osgoodms.com
To: AlbertJG@aol.com
November 30, 2007

Dear James

I've got my eye (not yet my hands) on a perfectly wonderful bundle of
fifteen Trollope letters – <u>really</u> meaty letters – all to the same
correspondent and with copies of this correspondent's own (clever
enough) letters to Trollope. Very special stuff. I'm technically not
supposed to be letting anyone in on this, so let's keep it strictly entre
nous for the time being.

Phillip

From: phil@osgoodms.com
To: gerald.lyons@hrc.utexas.edu
November 30, 2007

Dear Gerry

I am hoping to be able to offer for sale an extraordinary – and I mean
extraordinary – collection of some 110 letters, substantial, important
letters, from Dickens, Thackeray, George Eliot, Trollope, Hardy, Wilkie
Collins, Mrs. Gaskell, Butler, etc. These are letters to a Victorian
bookseller, which said bookseller has left us copies of all of his side of
the correspondence with these famous Victorians. I'd say, from a quick
perusal of them in photocopy, that nothing like them has come on the
market in years. The owner (a descendant of the bookseller) thinks to
auction them in some nine individual lots at Christie's London. My
thought is – if I can get them – that someplace like the Harry Ransom
might want the whole shebang.

Phillip

From: L.Dickerson@verizon.net
To: CharlieDover@christies.co.uk
Nov. 30, 2007

Dear Charlie

    Don't be angry with me, but that fellow who stopped by our table
at lunch has convinced me to send him a set of the photocopies for a
"second opinion." The minute I did it I had another second opinion of
my own, namely that I shouldn't have done this. I told him I was with
Christie's and had been for a year. Nothing has happened, really. But
I'm depressed. Say something nice to me.

                                        Yours
                                        Larry

From: CharlieDover@christies.co.uk
To: L.Dickerson@verizon.net
1 December 2007

Dear Larry

I can't say I am overjoyed to have someone else involved, but as long as
you have not agreed to anything or signed anything with him, I hope it
won't do any harm.

Yours
Charlie

From: L.Dickerson@verizon.net
To: CharlieDover@christies.co.uk
Dec. 1, 2007

    Jesus, Charlie, that's not a very forgiving letter.

From: CharlieDover@christies.co.uk
To: L.Dickerson@verizon.net
2 December 2007

Dear Larry

What can I say? Tell him you strictly forbid his showing them to
anybody else or telling anyone about them.

Charlie

⌒⌒

INTEROFFICE MEMO

From   Charlie Dover   Books and Manuscripts
To   Stephen Nicholls   Vice President
2 December 2007

Stephen

Look at these two emails. Phillip Osgood, no less, is somehow or other in the mix. What do you think?

Charlie

⌒⌒

INTEROFFICE MEMO

From   Stephen Nicholls   Vice President
To: Charlie Dover   Books and Manuscripts
2 December 2007

Charlie

My bet is Dickerson will be loyal.

Stephen

⌒⌒

From: phil@osgoodms.com
To: L.Dickerson@verizon.net
December 4, 2007

Dear Mr. Dickerson,

Your collection is immensely important and unusually unified – in spite of there being ten writers. That includes your great-great-grandfather. Has Christie's still not given estimates?

Yours truly
Phillip Osgood

⌣⟶

From: L.Dickerson@verizon.net
To: phil@osgoodms.com
Dec. 4, 2007

Dear Mr. Osgood,

   I have as yet no word on an estimate from London. I spent a year getting ready to send the copies to Christie's so I suppose I can wait a few days to hear from them.
   You must promise again not to show them to anybody or tell anybody about them.
   Stephen Nicholls long ago explained the strategy of keeping all the Dickens correspondence – both sides – together, all the Thackeray together, etc – nine batches or lots. Is that also your opinion? Nicholls also explained to me that the money was in the big boys and that my great-great-grandfather's letters were basically worthless, except as providing context.

                                            Yours
                                            Larry Dickerson

From: phil@osgoodms.com
To: L.Dickerson@verizon.net
December 4, 2007

Dear Mr. Dickerson,

Mum's the word unless you tell me otherwise. I do have clients, wealthy individuals as well as large institutions, who would surely be interested in particular lots, or even in the entire collection. But I'll hold off contacting them.

I concur with the nine-lots strategy, but <u>only after</u> an attempt to sell the entire archive has failed to bring a big-time buyer. An institution like the British Library might wish to buy the whole archive, by way of keeping (or regaining) part of the nation's heritage. Also, a wealthy place like the Harry Ransom Library in Texas might consider taking the whole thing. One advantage of the entire-archive-first approach over the nine-lots procedure is that with the nine-lots strategy there is always the possibility that one or two of the lots will not reach their minimum or reserve and there is no sale. You will see immediately that the two-step tactic is something a dealer like myself can undertake, whereas an auction house by its very nature cannot undertake to do so. They sell things one way or the other.

Moreover, to say that your great-great-grandfather's letters are basically worthless seems to me old-fashioned and <u>wrong</u>. In my view your ancestor's letters are in fact quite valuable, not only as providing context, but in themselves; scholars and collectors today are interested not merely in big names, but also – granted, to a lesser degree – in more ordinary people, including, naturally, booksellers. I grant of course that in a lot of, say, thirty Dickens/MacDowell letters, the chief value of the lot is in the Dickens letters. But the fact that we have letters (even though copies) of Dickens's correspondent, providing the wherewithal for determining just what Dickens is responding to, is very important. We cannot put a price (nor need we) on MacDowell's letters as separate entities (the way we could with separate Dickens letters), but, without question, having MacDowell's letters, having both side of the correspondence, adds very significantly to the value of this batch of Dickens letters.

Yours truly
Phillip Osgood

⟶

From: L.Dickerson@verizon.net
To: CharlieDover@christies.co.uk
Dec. 5, 2007

Dear Charlie

    As you can imagine, I'm holding my breath on the estimates.

Yours
Larry

⟶

From: CharlieDover@christies.co.uk
To: L.Dickerson@verizon.net
6 December 2007

Dear Larry

Here's a very rough preliminary estimate for the whole, in dollars, at the current exchange rate: $250,000 to $350,000. These, you understand, are estimates, not guarantees. We need to do some fine tuning on each of the nine lots. Shortly I shall send you a breakdown, i.e., high and low estimates for all nine lots, and toting up these nine sets of figures will probably come to, as I say, somewhere in the neighbourhood of $250,000 to $350,000, give or take as much as

$10,000 to $15,000. We have to examine the content of all these letters in making our determination of what estimates to set. When you have seen these and approve, we will send you a contract after the originals arrive in good condition here in London.

Yours
Charlie

From: L.Dickerson@verizon.net
To: CharlieDover@christies.co.uk
Dec. 6, 2007

   Charlie, $350,000! Sounds incredible! Larry

From: CharlieDover@christies.co.uk
To: L.Dickerson@verizon.net
7 December 2007

Dear Larry

Right, but you are of course counting on the high estimate. You should also bear in mind 1/ that at this point (as per my last) these are still <u>preliminary</u> estimates only; 2/ that your net gain will be subject to a vendor's commission (a negotiable percentage), but probably about 15%; and 3/ that there is the danger that certain lots will not meet your reserve, or minimum, and the items would not sell. For an item to fetch a truly high price at auction, there need to be, as we say, two birds fighting over one worm. If there is only one bird that seriously wants the worm – you see the point. The price bid stays low.

Yours
Charlie

From: L.Dickerson@verizon.net
To: CharlieDover@christies.co.uk
Dec. 7, 2007

Dear Charlie

　　Got it. But I'm still blown away.

　　　　　　　　　　　　　　　　Larry

From: L.Dickerson@verizon.net
To: phil@osgoodms.com
Dec. 7, 2007

Dear Mr. Osgood,

　　I almost hesitate to do this, but I'm forwarding to you what looks to me like Christie's estimate of what Christie's real estimate will be. Pretty shocking in any case.

　　　　　　　　　　　　　　　　Yours
　　　　　　　　　　　　　　　　Larry Dickerson

From: phil@osgoodms.com
To: L.Dickerson@verizon.net
December 9, 2007

Dear Mr. Dickerson,

I offer you $400,000 cash. Merry Christmas. Would you please come up to lunch and discuss the matter?

Yours truly
Phillip Osgood

⌒

From: L.Dickerson@verizon.net
To: phil@osgoodms.com
Dec. 9, 2007

Dear Mr. Osgood,

   You took the wind out of me. I don't know where I am, Let me think, I've been dealing with Christie's for so long. Let's hold off on lunch for a week or so.

Yours
Larry Dickerson

⌒

From: phil@osgoodms.com
To: L.Dickerson@verizon.net
December 9, 2007

Dear Mr. Dickerson or, if I may, Dear Larry,

I understand your dilemma. And I don't mean to hurry or pressure you.

But time does matter in arrangements like these. Come to lunch
Thursday at a place near me called Sette Mezzo, Lexington near East
70th Street, at 1 pm.

Yours truly
Phillip

From: L.Dickerson@verizon.net
To: CharlieDover@christies.co.uk
Dec. 9, 2007

Dear Charlie and Stephen

   Christ, I don't know where I'm at. That goddamned Osgood has
offered me $400K cash.

                                                    Larry

From: CharlieDover@christies.co.uk
To: L.Dickerson@verizon.net
10 December 2007

Dear Larry

I don't know what to say. Give me a few days to run through all the figures
again. But our numbers are estimates only. We can't outbid Osgood –
that, as you know, is not how auction houses obtain items to offer at
auction. We can't be disingenuous and say the total purchases may in fact
go to $400,000. Indeed they could, but we honestly don't think they will.

Yours
Charlie

From: L.Dickerson@verizon.net
To: phil@osgoodms.com
Dec. 10, 2007

Dear Phillip

　　I feel as if coming to lunch means it's a done deal, and it isn't. I feel committed to Christie's, especially to Stephen Nicholls and Charlie Dover.

                                               Yours
                                               Larry

From: phil@osgoodms.com
To: L.Dickerson@verizon.net
December 10, 2007

Dear Larry,

It's only lunch, I assure you.

Phillip

From: L.Dickerson@verizon.net
To: phil@osgoodms.com
Dec. 10, 2007

　　Okay. Thursday it is.

From: L.Dickerson@verizon.net
To: phil@osgoodms.com
Dec. 13, 2007

Dear Phillip

　　Thanks for lunch and all the good advice about publishing my book, etc. You made it clear you need a quick answer. Give me another 48 hours.

Yours
Larry

⌣⟶

From: L.Dickerson@verizon.net
To: Nicholls@btinternet.com
Dec. 13, 2007

Dear Stephen

　　I'm writing to you privately and over Charlie's head because this is an emergency. I'm sure she told you about this Osgood fellow and the offer he is making to me.

　　Do you – and Charlie – work on salary or on commission? I wouldn't want to be taking money out of your pockets. Jesus, I'm a wreck. This kind of stuff is not for me. It's all totally unreal. The idea of getting money should be making me happy – Christ, even $100,000 – even $50,000 or less would make me happy. But I'm not happy. I'm a mental wreck.

　　I had lunch with Osgood and he seemed to say he understood my problem, but he did say that he could not keep his offer open very long. Then he asked me if I had grandchildren. Two, I said. And he says, "Don't you want to leave them something nice?"

　　And he's lined up two interested "important big name" publishers for my transcriptions and notes.

I haven't said yes or no to him.

My conscience is bothering the hell out of me. I feel like a real shit (don't forward that word to Charlie).

Yours
Larry

⌒

From: Nicholls@btinternet.com
To: L.Dickerson@verizon.net
14 December 2007

Larry

Christie's employees are salaried, though sometimes a bonus might be paid at the end of the year for an employee who closes on a very big contract.

Stephen

⌒

From: L.Dickerson@verizon.net
To: Nicholls@btinternet.com
Dec. 14, 2007

Would this be a big contract?

⌒

From: Nicholls@btinternet.com
To: L.Dickerson@verizon.net
14 December 2007

Dear Larry

It's big and it's not big: We handle twelfth-century illuminated manuscripts, Leonardo da Vinci manuscript pages, even the occasional Gutenberg Bible. These are of a different order of magnitude from your letters. Your letters, on the other hand, represent a big contract as far as Victorian novelists' letters are concerned.

Stephen

From: L.Dickerson@verizon.net
To: Nicholls@btinternet.com
Dec. 14, 2007

Dear Stephen

    You know that's an ambiguous answer. Even I know that. If I jumped ship, would I be taking money from you?

                                            Larry

From: Nicholls@btinternet.com
To: L.Dickerson@verizon.net
14 December 2007

Dear Larry

That's the kind of information we are not supposed to reveal. Charlie and I would hate to lose you. That's all I can tell you.

Stephen

⟶

From: L.Dickerson@verizon.net
To: Nicholls@btinternet.com
Dec. 15, 2007

Dear Stephen

Jesus, I feel bad about this. Say something.

Larry

⟶

From: Nicholls@btinternet.com
To: L.Dickerson@verizon.net
15 December 2007

Larry

What can I say? Tell me again, has Osgood really offered $400,000 cash, no strings attached?

Stephen

From: L.Dickerson@verizon.net
To: Nicholls@btinternet.com
Dec. 15, 2007

Stephen

$400,000 cash on the barrel head.

You ask what can you say? You can say I'm a traitor, especially after all those months of you walking me through this new game. An ingrate, a real horse's ass, as we say.

Larry

From: Nicholls@btinternet.com
To: L.Dickerson@verizon.net
15 December 2007

Larry

I won't say you are any of those things. If you were, you would have taken Osgood's offer a week ago, immediately, without checking back with us.

You have your own interests, and I suppose you must look to them. As your fellow American John Updike puts it, "We all carry our own hides to market."

Stephen

From: L.Dickerson@verizon.net
To: Nicholls@btinternet.com
Dec. 15, 2007

Dear Stephen

I don't altogether understand the hides to market thing but I do get
your point. You're being too decent about this.

Larry

From: Nicholls@btinternet.com
To: L.Dickerson@verizon.net
16 December 2007

Dear Larry

I'm being honest. Our highest estimate is $350,000. If we weren't acting
honestly, we could put the high estimate at $500,000 and say we
hoped you would get to that figure. But we won't do that.

If I were not a Christie's employee but just a friend, I'd advise you to
take the money.

Yours
Stephen

From: L.Dickerson@verizon.net
To: Nicholls@btinternet.com
Dec. 16, 2007

Dear Stephen

    Christ, you are a prince. And Charlie is a princess. I'll deal further with Osgood and see the color of his money before doing anything drastic.

Larry

From: L.Dickerson@verizon.net
To: Nicholls@btinternet.com
Jan. 2, 2008

Stephen

    Jesus, I've deposited a $400,000 bank check into my account! I hope you forgive me.

Larry

From: Nicholls@btinternet.com
To: L.Dickerson@verizon.net
6 April 2008

Dear Larry

How are you?

I know you'll be relieved to learn that some of your chickens, so to
speak, are coming home to roost. Or at least most of them. Osgood has
been in touch with Charlie, saying he hopes there are no hard feelings
at Christie's: "It's just business." He was not able to sell the entire
archive for a profit (though he hinted the British Library and the Harry
Ransom Library came close). So he's selling through us the remaining
lots of the individual authors – as had been our intent. He claims he
has done "exceptionally well" with Trollope (apparently Princeton Rare
Books and a wealthy Wall Streeter vied with each other almost to the
death). He also did "surprisingly" well with the Darwin – Darwin has
been so much in the news – and the buyer took at a "good price" the
Butler letters because of the evolution connection. So now Osgood is
offering Christie's the remaining authors to put at auction for him:
Dickens, Thackeray, Eliot, Hardy, Collins, and Gaskell. In regard to the
Dickens, Osgood has been in touch with two prospective "very high"
bidders; and he has spoken with a "fanatical" Thackeray collector who,
like the two Dickens bidders, insists on buying at auction rather than
from a dealer. The upshot is that Osgood is confident he will come out
ahead and that Christie's should really not do too poorly either – six of
the nine lots having ended up back here. The sale will be in the late
spring. I hope this salves your (still?) slightly troubled conscience.

Yours ever
And best

Stephen

From: L.Dickerson@verizon.net
To: Nicholls@btinternet.com
April 6, 2008

Dear Stephen

So good to hear from you. Hello to Charlie.

Christ Almighty, that is the best news I've had in a long time. Certainly the best since I nervously deposited $400,000 into my bank account. And, as you know, still feeling kind of guilty about it. But you know what? With this windfall in my pocket, after what you just told me, I'm seriously thinking of bidding on one batch of letters — maybe the George Eliot letters, or the Hardy, since you say some "very high" bidders already have their eyes on Dickens and Thackeray. But me having 400K in the bank, I might very well bid — and that would be a new experience and fun for me — on the George Eliot or Hardy letters. Then, as they say here in real estate, I would "flip" them in your next auction.

Yours
Larry

ABOUT THE AUTHOR

N. JOHN HALL is Distinguished Professor of English at Bronx
Community College and the Graduate Center, City University of New
York. The recipient of numerous awards, he has had fellowships from
the National Endowment for the Humanities, the American Council
of Learned Societies, and twice from the Guggenheim Foundation.
He is considered one of the world's leading authorities on Anthony
Trollope and Max Beerbohm. His publications include *Trollope and
His Illustrators* (Macmillan, 1980); *The Letters of Anthony Trollope*
(Stanford, 1983); *Trollope: A Biography* (Oxford, 1991); *Max Beerbohm
Caricatures* (Yale, 1997); *Max Beerbohm: A Kind of a Life* (Yale, 2002);
and *Belief: A Memoir* (Beil, 2007). Since 1967 he has lived in Greenwich
Village, New York.

A NOTE ON THE TYPE

CORRESPONDENCE *has been set in Mentor Sans Pro Light, a type designed by Michael Harvey. One member of a family of types whose evolution began in the 1970s – when Harvey created lettering for book illustrations – Mentor reappeared on book jackets in the 1990s, evolving slowly into the present types, which are available in a variety of weights in both serif and sans-serif faces. Readable at text sizes and elegant at display sizes, the Mentor types reveal Harvey's close study of the work of Eric Gill, Reynolds Stone, and Hermann Zapf.*

DESIGN & COMPOSITION BY CARL W. SCARBROUGH